"Chris is a Sheridan . . . stubborn and proud just like his father and grandfather before him,"

Vienna said evenly. "Don't you see that, Drew? Your son wants to trust you, to love you—" her throat clogged with emotion "—but you have to earn that trust."

Drew's jaw tightened, and his eyes stared unseeingly at her. Suddenly she had the strongest urge to reach out and smooth away the tension on his face, to kiss away the lines of strain near his strong, sensual mouth.

"Why?" Drew asked softly, his dark eyes holding hers. "Why do you care so much, Vienna, about Chris...? Or, for that matter, me?"

Dear Reader,

Happy holidays! Though it may be cold outside, it's always warmed by the festivities of this special season. Everyone at Silhouette Books wishes you joy and cheer at this wonderful time of the year.

In December, we have some heartwarming books to take the chill off the weather. The final title in our DIAMOND JUBILEE celebration is *Only the Nanny Knows for Sure* by Phyllis Halldorson. Don't miss this tender love story about a nanny who has a secret . . . and a handsome hero who doesn't stand a ghost of a chance at remaining a bachelor!

The DIAMOND JUBILEE—Silhouette Romance's tenth anniversary celebration—is our way of saying thanks to you, our readers. To symbolize the timelessness of love, as well as the modern gift of the tenth anniversary, we've presented readers with a DIAMOND JUBILEE Silhouette Romance each month in 1990, penned by one of your favorite Silhouette Romance authors. It's been a wonderful year of love and romance here at Silhouette Books, and we hope that you've enjoyed our DIAMOND JUBILEE celebration. Saying thanks has never been so much fun!

And that's not all! There are six books a month from Silhouette Romance—stories by wonderful writers who time and time again bring home the magic of love. And we've got a lot of exciting events planned for 1991. In January, look for Marie Ferrarella's *The Undoing of Justin Starbuck*—the first book in the WRITTEN IN THE STARS series. Each month in 1991, we're proud to present readers with a book that focuses on the hero—and his Zodiac sign. Be sure to watch for that mysterious Capricorn man . . . and then meet Mr. Aquarius in *Man from the North Country* by Laurie Paige in February.

1991 is sure to be extra special. With works by authors such as Diana Palmer (don't miss her upcoming Long, Tall Texan!), Annette Broadrick, Nora Roberts and so many other talented writers, how could it not be? It's always celebration time at Silhouette Romance—the celebration of love.

I hope you'll enjoy this book and all of the stories to come. Come home to romance—Silhouette Romance—for always!

Sincerely,

Tara Gavin
Senior Editor

MOYRA TARLING

Just in Time for Christmas

Published by Silhouette Books New York

America's Publisher of Contemporary Romance

To my husband, Noel,
with all my love, always.

My thanks to Margo Jacobsen, D.V.M.,
for taking the time to answer my questions.

SILHOUETTE BOOKS
300 E. 42nd St., New York, N.Y. 10017

ISBN: 0-373-08763-2

First Silhouette Books printing December 1990

MOYRA TARLING

is the youngest of four children born and raised in Aberdeenshire, Scotland. It was there that she was first introduced to and became hooked on romance novels.

After emigrating to Vancouver, Canada, Ms. Tarling met her future husband, Noel, at a party in Birch Bay—and promptly fell in love. They now have two children. Together they enjoy browsing through antique shops and auctions, looking for various items, from old gramophones to antique corkscrews and buttonhooks.

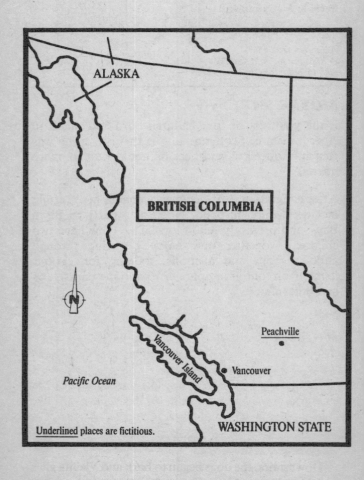

ALASKA

BRITISH COLUMBIA

Peachville

Vancouver Island

Vancouver

Pacific Ocean

Underlined places are fictitious.

WASHINGTON STATE

Chapter One

Vienna sank deeper into the warm water of the bath and closed her eyes. It felt so good to relax and let her worries drift away on the soapy tide of bubbles clinging to the tub.

Tobias was going to be fine—the doctors had said so. He was over the worst and was beginning, thank God, to recover from the heart attack that had struck him down less than a week ago. She'd come home from the clinic and found him on the floor. Luckily she'd arrived just in time.

The image of Tobias lying facedown on the carpet crystallized in her mind and Vienna opened her eyes and blinked it away. He was going to be all right—he had to be. He was her godfather, and the only family she had left in the world.

Downstairs, the dogs began to bark and Vienna gave a sigh as she eased herself out of the water and reached for the towel. With quick, deft movements she dried herself and slipped into the white terry-cloth bathrobe she kept on the hook behind the door.

Since taking over Bill Logan's veterinary practice a little over a year ago, she had quickly come to realize that the folks in town who still brought their pets to her assumed that in an emergency they could bring their animals to the house.

Her short, dark curls glistened with dampness as she hurried down the stairs. Glancing at the clock in the hallway, she saw that it was nearly ten o'clock.

"Buffy...Daisy...it's all right. Quiet, now. Good dogs," she told them in a firm voice as she made her way down the dimly lit hall toward the front door.

Buffy, the small white poodle, raced to the chair by the window and, jumping up, put her small paws on the sill. Daisy, the big black Labrador, continued to bark. Pushing her aside with her knee, Vienna opened the door.

Her heart skidded to a halt and a kaleidoscope of memories and emotions cascaded over her at the sight of Drew Sheridan standing in the doorway. He seemed so tall, so overpowering, so devastatingly male that she had to fight the urge to shut the door and lock it. But Daisy was already rubbing herself against Drew's legs, her tail wagging a welcome that would have made any burglar laugh.

"You came," Vienna said huskily as she stared into eyes that were black as night and equally as mysterious—eyes she'd seen a thousand times in her dreams, eyes she'd never thought she'd see again.

"We came." His voice was deep and slightly raspy and the sound of it stirred the hairs on the back of her neck.

"We?" she repeated, bending to grab Daisy's collar. As she did so, the tie on her robe loosened, giving the man a brief glimpse of one creamy white breast. Fumbling, Vienna quickly covered herself and tried to ignore the rush of heat that crept over her face.

"Do you always answer the door half-naked?" Drew asked, his voice cutting through the haze of emotions that had swamped her the moment she'd opened the door to him.

"Not always," she managed, annoyed at his tone. "Aren't you coming in?"

"I just wanted to make sure there was someone here to let us in. I'll get Christopher," he said, and turning on his heel, he disappeared down the front steps.

Now that his tall frame was no longer shielding her, the chilly December air swirled around Vienna and she drew the robe tighter. Christopher? Who was Christopher?

She peered into the darkness, but all she could see was the shape of the taxi outlined against the night sky. Leaving the door ajar, she turned and strode purposefully down the hall. Taking the steps two at a time, she ran up to her bedroom.

She tossed the robe on the bed, then grabbed a sweatshirt and jeans from the chair and as she pulled them on she recalled Drew's penetrating gaze when her robe had slithered open. A flash of heat swept through her once more, and annoyed, she thrust her feet into a pair of slippers. Without bothering to look in the mirror, she dashed from the room.

She was halfway down the stairs when he appeared at the bottom, carrying a small sleeping child.

"Where shall I put him?" he asked, already beginning to climb the steps.

The sight of Drew with a child in his arms startled Vienna, and she hesitated slightly before responding. "Your old room will be fine. There are two single beds in there now . . . or there's the small room. . . ."

"My old room is fine."

Vienna nodded, and retracing her steps, she led the way to the bedroom next to hers. It was fairly spacious and had two twin beds, a single dresser, a small night table, several old armchairs, and a walk-in closet.

Instead of switching on the bright overhead light, she leaned across to the bedside lamp and suddenly the room was bathed in a muted glow. Straightening, she turned and almost collided with Drew and his cargo.

"Sorry . . . I'll get out of your way." She moved aside, but not before she managed a glance at the sleeping child in Drew Sheridan's arms. The boy had to be about five or six years old, Vienna guessed, and the resemblance to Drew was uncanny.

There was little doubt that he was Drew's son—Drew and Natalie's son, she amended, and this thought brought a sharp stab of pain near the region of her heart. "I'll make a pot of coffee," she said, preparing to leave.

"I told the taxi driver to put the suitcases inside the door," Drew said quietly as he gently laid the boy on the bed. "I'll take care of them in a minute," he added, without turning around.

Slowly Vienna descended the stairs, her thoughts on the child. If Christopher was Drew's son, then he was also Tobias's grandson...a grandson he'd known nothing about.

Anger exploded inside her. How could Drew have deprived Tobias of the knowledge he had a grandson? Surely he could have put aside the resentment he felt toward his father and let the old man know!

Vienna knew just how much having a grandchild would have meant to Tobias, and her heart hardened a little against the man upstairs.

The dogs met her at the foot of the stairs and followed her into the kitchen. Vienna crossed to the back door. "Out you go, you two. Last call," she said as they trotted outside.

She moved to the sink and began to fill the coffee-pot, reminding herself that it wasn't any of her business what Drew Sheridan did. But if it wasn't any of her business, then why had she taken it upon herself to call him in California the day after Tobias's heart attack?

It had only been this past year that she'd discovered, purely by accident, Drew's whereabouts. She'd been reading an article in a business magazine when she'd suddenly noticed a photograph of him.

She'd have known him anywhere—those dark, brooding looks, those eyes that even from the photograph seemed to pierce right through her. Beneath the picture was a caption stating that Drew Sheridan of

Sheridan Electronics, California, had recently bought out a small electronics firm in Oregon.

Later, in the privacy of her room, she'd scanned the pages, hoping to discover more, but the photograph and the caption were all she could find.

She hadn't shown it to Tobias. Any mention of Drew was generally met with stony silence. Over the years, the rift between father and son had grown too wide to cross. Suddenly, she found herself wondering just what kind of reaction Tobias would have upon learning that Drew had come home.

"The coffee smells good."

Vienna jumped at the sound of Drew's voice and tried to ignore the way her pulse quickened in response.

Turning from the stove, she watched him approach the kitchen table. He'd removed his heavy overcoat and was wearing a pair of navy slacks and a dark green pullover sweater atop a white polo-neck shirt.

He looked stunning. His black hair had a wind-swept look, as if he'd only moments before run his hand through it, and his eyes were dark and sultry, fanned by incredibly long, jet-black lashes. His face had a lean, mean, arrogant look that sent a shiver up her spine.

"It's almost ready," Vienna managed, turning back to the stove to adjust the controls and lower the heat.

"Is my father..." Drew stopped, unable to complete the question.

"Tobias is doing fine," she answered calmly, turning to face him once more. "It was touch and go at the start—that's why I called you. But earlier today, the doctors told me they're sure he'll pull through.''

Drew lowered himself into one of the old wooden kitchen chairs, unable to quite fathom the feeling of relief sweeping through him.

The telephone call he'd received from Vienna less than a week ago, telling him his father had suffered a heart attack and might not live, had shaken him more than he'd thought possible. It had been a little over eight years since he'd seen his father—since he'd last set foot in this house—but suddenly it seemed like only yesterday.

He took a steadying breath as his glance traveled around the familiar room. He couldn't help noticing that there were quite a few changes, all noticeably feminine. Then his eyes came to rest on Vienna, taking in the short dark curls, the gray eyes that held more than a hint of censure.

"Does he know that you called me?'' Drew asked and knew instantly by the way she fumbled with the coffee mug that she hadn't told his father she'd made the call.

"No, he doesn't know,'' she replied as she carried the two steaming mugs to the table.

"I see.'' Drew's comment brought her eyes to focus on his.

"I thought it might upset him,'' she said, taking the seat near him. "And the doctors told me he needed absolute quiet—no stress of any kind, complete rest. Besides, you didn't exactly give me the impression that you were coming,'' she added, remembering the rather awkward silence she'd encountered when she'd told him why she was calling.

His head came up abruptly and a blaze of anger danced in the dark depths of his eyes. "Eight years ago my father ordered me out of this house and told me he never wanted to see me again. You were there, you should remember," he said in a tone edged with ice. "Forgive me if I wasn't all warmth and charm on the telephone, but the news you imparted came as quite a shock."

"I'm sorry," she responded quickly. "I just reacted, I guess—when they said they weren't sure he'd survive...." Emotions were suddenly clawing at her throat and she had to blink back the tears threatening to overwhelm her.

His hand came out to cover hers, and Vienna was unprepared for the jolt of heat that raced along her arm, and equally astonished at the way her pulse seemed to dance at his touch. "I'm sorry...I didn't mean to snap at you. I've had rather a hectic few days, and then I wasn't sure I'd get here in time." Drew's voice faded and as he held her gaze, she was aware of something strange happening inside her.

She eased her hand from beneath his on the pretext of reaching for the sugar bowl and spoon. With deliberate movements, she added sugar to her coffee and slowly stirred it. "I guess we're both a little overwrought," she said, careful to keep her eyes averted from his. "How old is...Christopher?" she asked, hoping a change of subject would ease the tension.

"What? Oh! He's seven," Drew replied.

"He looks remarkably like you," she said. She lifted her glance to meet his and was surprised to see his expression darken. His mouth tightened, and his eyes hardened to look like glittering pieces of black coal.

"That was my impression the first time I saw him," Drew told her. His fingers gripped the handle of the mug as he remembered opening the door of his apartment six months ago to find himself looking down at the face of a small boy he knew instantly to be his.

Vienna tried to smile, but she could sense that somehow, unknowingly, she had stepped on an open wound. "He looked like you when he was born?" she ventured, not sure why she was pursuing the subject, but unable now to let it go.

"That, I couldn't tell you," Drew answered brusquely as he rose from the chair. "I'm rather tired. I think I'll go to bed. What time are visiting hours at the hospital?"

"There's no restriction when it comes to immediate family," she told him. "But I'm not sure—"

"I didn't come all this way not to see him," Drew cut in, impatience evident in his voice. Vienna blinked in surprise. Drew had spoken in the exact tone and manner his father often used. The similarities were so striking that for a moment, she almost smiled.

"Of course you should see him," she agreed quickly. "And I know he'll be thrilled when he sees Christopher. It's just that, I think perhaps I should go with you, to prepare him...."

"All right," Drew said, accepting her reasoning. He certainly didn't want his sudden appearance to cause his father to have another attack.

The sound of scratching at the kitchen door caused them both to glance in that direction. Vienna moved to let the dogs in. They ran immediately toward Drew, tails wagging and noses sniffing.

"Mutt and Jeff," he said as he bent to pat both dogs.

"Daisy and Buffy," Vienna corrected, and at the sound of their names the two dogs returned to her side.

"You always did have a way with animals," Drew mused. A small smile curled at the edges of his mouth as he watched the dogs gaze adoringly at Vienna. "Did you pursue your dream and make it through veterinary college?" he asked, his eyes sparkling with interest and amusement.

"Yes," she said, a note of pride in her voice. "But it would still only be a dream if it wasn't for your father." Her words effectively swept the smile from Drew's face.

"It's unfortunate that I can't say the same," he said in a voice that held more than a trace of bitterness. Before she could speak he went on. "I'll say goodnight. Christopher is an early riser. Thanks for the coffee," he added before turning and making his way from the room.

Vienna stared after him for a long moment. Not until she felt Daisy's cold wet nose against her hand did she move.

"All right, girls. Bedtime," she told them and crossed to the small room off the kitchen where the dogs spent the night.

Vienna spent the next five minutes tidying up the kitchen. She lingered there, listening to the sound of water running in the bathroom and making no move to go to her own room until she heard Drew's bedroom door close.

She was still finding it difficult to believe that he'd actually come. Though she wasn't at all sure what kind of reaction his father would have to seeing Drew, she knew that Christopher's presence would be exactly the kind of surprise Tobias needed. A grandchild! The old man's dream had come true.

But what about Natalie—Christopher's mother? Had she refused to come? There had never been any love lost between Natalie and Tobias. She had played a significant role in the drama that had unfolded that summer a little over eight years ago, and had taken great pleasure in antagonizing Tobias, who'd made no bones about the fact that he heartily disapproved of her relationship with Drew. That in itself could easily explain Natalie's absence. It had been on the tip of her tongue to ask Drew if his wife would be joining him, but she'd refrained.

She and Natalie had never quite hit it off, either. But that had been because Natalie had guessed Vienna's secret—that she'd had a terrible crush on Drew.

But Drew, six years her senior, had looked upon Vienna as a younger sister and perhaps as a friend—but nothing more.

At this thought, a pain caught at Vienna's heart and she silently chided herself for letting an old memory get the better of her. Eight years was a long time, and her feelings for Drew had long since faded and died.

All was quiet when she locked the back door and slowly made her way upstairs to her room. There were no sounds coming from the next room. As she closed her bedroom door, she tried to imagine what Tobias would say when the three of them arrived at the hospital in the morning.

Always an early riser, Vienna was in the kitchen making pancakes when she heard a sound behind her. Standing in the doorway, wearing a white T-shirt and blue jeans, was Drew's son.

"Good morning, Christopher," she greeted him. "My name's Vienna. How are you this morning?"

"Okay," came the shy reply.

"I've made pancakes for breakfast. Would you like some?"

"Yes, please," he said, but made no move to venture farther into the kitchen.

Vienna turned back to the stove and, taking the spatula, she scooped the three pancakes from the frying pan and slid them onto a plate. Plate in hand, she turned back toward him and her heart gave a flutter when she saw Drew appear behind the boy. He wore a pale blue sweater atop a crisp white shirt and black jeans. His hair was still damp from the shower and shone like polished ebony. He casually swept a glance over her gray slacks and pale pink sweater, and the look sent a shiver chasing along her spine.

"Good morning," she said, a hint of breathlessness in her voice. "I was just asking Christopher if he liked pancakes."

"I think they're one of his favorites," Drew replied. "Let's sit at the table, shall we?" He addressed the young boy, who was looking rather apprehensively at his father.

"He says you have two dogs," Christopher said, with a nod in his father's direction. "Where are they?" He climbed onto a kitchen chair.

Vienna frowned as she glanced from father to son. The atmosphere between them could only be described as strained, and Vienna was suddenly reminded of past meals she'd shared at this table with Tobias and Drew. The atmosphere then had been even more tense and uncomfortable.

Was Christopher here under protest? she wondered. Had the little boy wanted to stay with his mother?

"Yes, I have two dogs," she told him. "They're outside at the moment. I usually leave them there until after breakfast, as they're always getting in my way. I hope you like dogs," she added, suddenly wondering if perhaps that was the problem.

"I love dogs." Christopher was quick to respond. "And I'm going to ask Santa to bring me a puppy for Christmas, so I can have a dog of my very own." His tone was almost defiant.

"Chris..." Drew cautioned. "I've already explained to you that animals aren't allowed in my apartment block. It's a rule. Besides, owning a puppy is a big responsibility."

Vienna set the plate in front of Chris, wondering all the while at the familiar tone of the conversation going on between father and son.

"Your father's right, Chris. Dogs are a lot of work to look after," Vienna pointed out, trying to ease the tension in the air. "And after the Christmas holidays are over and you go back to school, and your father goes back to work, it's your mother who will be the one looking after the puppy until you get home," she continued.

Her words were met with a deathly silence, and instantly Vienna knew she'd said something wrong.

"I don't have a mommy anymore," Christopher said in a voice that was so lacking in emotion, Vienna's heart went out to him. Her glance flew to Drew, and the fierce expression she saw on his face spoke of anger.

"I'm sorry..." she faltered. "I didn't know—"

"Natalie died a year ago," Drew informed her as he sat down.

Vienna's thoughts were in chaos as she turned to the stove and opened the oven door. Extracting a plate laden with pancakes, she turned and set it in the middle of the table.

She sat down opposite Drew, trying with difficulty to absorb the news. Natalie was dead. Beautiful, willful Natalie was dead. Vienna couldn't believe it, and she found the reactions of the two sitting at the table unusual, to say the least. There seemed to be no sign of sadness, no sign of the grief generally associated with the kind of loss they'd suffered. Were they simply good at hiding their feelings? she wondered. But recalling the matter-of-fact way the boy had spoken, she felt a shiver chase down her spine. There were so many questions she wanted to ask, but glancing at the two figures seated at the table with her, she sensed that the topic of Natalie was taboo.

"After breakfast we're going into town to the hospital to visit my father, your grandfather," Drew said a few moments later.

"Do I have to?" Chris asked, pushing his food around the plate.

"Yes, you have to." Drew's voice held a note of exasperation, and Vienna frowned. Something wasn't right here—she could feel it. The two people seated at the table were behaving like strangers. It didn't make sense. Had Natalie's death caused a rift between them?

"Your grandfather will be thrilled to see you, Chris," Vienna said, and smiled warmly at the boy.

"Why?" Chris asked, and to Vienna, his tone implied that no one had ever been thrilled with him in his whole life.

Vienna was tempted for a moment to cast a questioning glance at Drew, but she kept her eyes on Chris, sensing that her answer was of ultimate importance to the boy.

"Tobias—that's your grandfather—has always wanted a grandson, and as you're his first and only grandchild, you'll always be very special to him." Vienna watched as Chris carefully considered her words. She couldn't help thinking that he seemed unusually serious for someone who was only seven years old. Again a flurry of questions came into her head.

"He'll be the only grandfather I have," Chris said at last. "That's pretty special, too, isn't it?" he asked, a small spark lighting his dark, knowing eyes.

"Yes, it is," Vienna said softly.

Chris's face broke into a wide smile and her heart melted at the dramatic change in his appearance. Gone was the wariness, the seriousness that seemed to surround him, and Vienna realized intuitively that Chris wasn't a child who smiled easily or often. But he'd smiled at her, and she couldn't stop the warmth that spread through her at this thought.

"Can I go outside now and see the dogs?" Chris suddenly asked.

His question was directed at Vienna, and again she found herself wondering at the boy's relationship with his father. This time she glanced at Drew, and at his nod of approval she turned back to Chris.

"Yes, go ahead," she said. "But you'll need a warm jacket or coat. It's supposed to snow today."

"Oh, boy!" Chris's smile was again dazzling.

Vienna returned the smile, for she, too, loved snow. "The dogs' names are Daisy and Buffy," she explained. "Daisy is the black one—she's big but she wouldn't hurt a fly."

"Your jacket is upstairs on the bed, Chris. You should probably wear a hat...but I don't think I brought one," Drew said.

"There are a couple of toques on the seat by the front door," Vienna told him. "Just grab one of those."

"Okay," Christopher said, but as he hopped from the chair, he neither glanced in his father's direction nor acknowledged his words.

Vienna rose from her chair, took the coffeepot from the stove, and filled the two cups on the table.

Drew broke the silence. "I suppose you're wondering why Chris hardly pays attention to me."

Vienna lifted her cup and took a sip of the hot liquid. Setting the cup back in its saucer, she spoke. "I must admit your relationship with him does seem rather unusual...."

"Then allow me to put you in the picture," he continued. "Chris arrived on my doorstep six months ago. Prior to that, I wasn't aware I even had a son."

"But, I thought..." Vienna began, but one look from Drew caused her to fall silent.

"When Natalie and I left here eight years ago, we stopped off in Reno on our way to Los Angeles and got married. And just as my father predicted, the marriage didn't last. Less than six months later, she walked out. She found a rich man—a man who could give her all the things I couldn't afford."

Drew closed his eyes for a moment as his thoughts flew back in time. Running away with Natalie had simply been an act of rebellion. His father had given him an ultimatum, telling him he had to choose between him and Natalie. Leaving with Natalie had seemed the only solution, but by the time they reached Los Angeles, he had come to realize that his feelings for Natalie had nothing to do with love. She'd been the means by which he was able to walk away from his father and show his independence. He'd used her—but

Natalie had also used him. She believed he would be her ticket to a better life.

Drew shook his head and quickly brought his thoughts back to the present. "What I didn't know," he continued, "was that when she left me, she was pregnant." He stood abruptly, almost knocking the chair over. "I never saw her again. Six months ago I was contacted by a lawyer in New York, telling me that Natalie had died in a car crash. The papers found in her dingy little apartment indicated that the boy who'd been left with a neighbor was my son. It had taken them months to track me down, and in the meantime Chris had been put in a foster home."

Drew was silent for a long moment. The memory of that phone call still lingered. He'd never known such anger. How could Natalie have kept such a secret? She'd had no right to deprive him of his son!

Drew turned to Vienna, but she wasn't sure he was even aware of her presence. "The lawyer flew out with Chris to California," he went on. "By then, I'd convinced myself that Natalie had lied about the child and that he couldn't possibly be mine...but when I saw the boy, I knew without a doubt he was my son."

Vienna felt her heart contract in pain. How could Natalie have been so cruel? How could she have hurt Drew like that? She, who in this very room had loudly proclaimed her love for Drew, and had smiled with smug satisfaction when they'd walked out together...

"I signed the necessary papers, and suddenly I had a son. But we were total strangers, and since then, things haven't exactly gone smoothly." Drew sighed and brought his gaze to meet hers. "End of story," he said with a shrug that belied the inner turmoil she could see shimmering in the depths of his blue-black eyes.

"It must have been quite a shock to discover you had a child," Vienna said, sympathy and understanding warming her tone as she stood and began to clear away the dishes.

"To say the least," he agreed. "Anyway, it's my problem. I felt I should explain."

"Chris must have been equally bewildered by the whole thing," Vienna commented carefully. "It will just take time for both of you to adjust."

"Time!" Drew spat the word out. "That's what everyone keeps telling me. But how much time?" He ran a hand through his hair and a faraway look came into his eyes. "Sometimes I wonder if he'll ever accept the fact that I'm his father."

Compassion for Drew tore through her at the pain she could hear in his voice. That the hurt ran deep was evident, and Vienna suddenly found herself wishing there was something she could do. Instinctively, she moved to stand before him, her sole purpose simply to comfort.

Gently, she took his hands in hers. The jolt of awareness that suddenly sped along her arms almost made her gasp aloud. Her eyes flew to his, and for an instant she saw something flicker in their black depths, but it was gone as quickly as it had come, making her wonder if she'd merely imagined it.

The air between them was alive with tension, and the warmth of his fingers curled around hers was doing strange things to her heart.

She swallowed and somehow found her voice. "Don't give up, Drew," she said. "Things will work out. You just have to believe it."

A cynical smile touched the corners of his mouth, and removing his hands from hers, he took several steps back. "Unfortunately, simply believing something will happen doesn't amount to a hill of beans—" He stopped, then mumbled under his breath.

He crossed to the back door, then turned to her once more. "I'll round up Chris. Then maybe we should head for the hospital, although I'm beginning to think that coming here was a mistake . . . a big mistake."

Chapter Two

Vienna watched in silence as Drew opened the kitchen door and disappeared outside. He had sounded bitter, cynical and utterly devoid of hope. But after hearing the explanation he'd given her concerning Christopher's arrival in his life, she could easily understand and sympathize.

He had every right to his anger and bitterness, but she knew that unless Drew put those feelings behind him, unless he found a way to reach Christopher, the relationship between him and his son would grow steadily worse.

As she cleared away the dishes, Vienna's thoughts suddenly switched to Drew's relationship with his father. It was somehow ironic that both sets of father and son were estranged. And as her thoughts shifted to Tobias, she found herself wondering just how he was going to react when she told him about Drew.

Eight years ago, she had watched helplessly as the two most important people in her life had fought a battle of wills—a battle she'd known neither could win. Tobias had made it abundantly clear to Drew that he disapproved of his association with Natalie Kent. He'd told his son continually that he should spend more time learning about the business he would one day inherit, instead of frittering his life away on a gold-digging tramp.

Tobias's high-handed attitude had simply fueled the fires of Drew's discontent, and she'd seen the resentment and anger slowly building in him. She'd tried to talk to Drew to soothe the troubled waters, but her efforts had been in vain. Drew told her he resented his father's demands on his time and felt stifled by the way Tobias seemed to have his life all mapped out for him without bothering to consult him.

Sympathetic to Drew's situation, Vienna had tried to talk to Tobias to make him see that he was slowly pushing his son away. But Tobias had stubbornly refused to listen to her, convinced that he knew what was best for Drew. In the final confrontation he'd forced Drew to make a choice. Drew had chosen Natalie.

But surely the fact that Drew was here now showed that he still cared about his father. Vienna could only pray that Tobias would put aside his foolish pride and simply welcome his son home.

Before she could contemplate further, the kitchen door suddenly opened, allowing Daisy and Buffy, tails wagging and mouths panting, to come running in. Behind them, smiling and gasping for breath, came Christopher and then Drew.

Christopher's cheeks were pink, and his eyes, so like Drew's, were bright and sparkling with joy and laughter.

"I won! I won!" cried Chris, grinning now. "I beat you Da—" Abruptly the boy stopped and the smile disappeared from his face.

Drew's smile vanished too, and he bit back a sigh. A few moments ago Chris had been chattering excitedly to him, telling him about Buffy and Daisy. Chris had acted and reacted like a normal, happy child, and for the first time since he'd arrived on Drew's doorstep, they had shared a moment together that was neither tense nor antagonistic.

It hadn't mattered in the least to Drew that his first real exchange with Chris had been about the dogs. All that had mattered was that it had happened. And when Drew challenged the boy to a race back to the house, Chris had actually grinned with delight—an action that had stirred to life the dying embers of Drew's hope.

Vienna quickly filled the silence. "I think the dogs won. You were next, Chris, and your father was last." For her efforts, she saw a small smile reappear on the boy's face.

"You beat me, all right," Drew said, his tone a shade too eager. "We'll have to have a rematch, Chris. What do you say?"

Vienna's heart was in her throat as she noted Drew's taut features. Chris hesitated, obviously uncertain what to do or say, and Vienna silently prayed he'd be kind. She sensed the boy's pain, and his fear, and she found herself wondering just what kind of life the youngster had had with Natalie, and why he seemed determined to keep his father at arm's length.

The silence stretched, and once again Vienna came to their rescue. "Chris? Did you know your father won all kinds of ribbons and trophies for running when he was in school?"

Chris turned to Vienna, a spark of interest lighting up those blue eyes. "He did?"

"He sure did!" Vienna kept her tone light. "Your grandfather used to talk about it all the time," she said, deliberately keeping her eyes on Chris. "They're in a storage box in the attic. Maybe you'd like to take a look at them sometime."

"That'd be neat," Chris replied. He glanced tentatively at Drew, as if expecting him to refuse.

"I'd forgotten about those," Drew said, a smile curling at his mouth. "Maybe we could take a look in the attic for them later." He was careful to keep the invitation casual.

"Okay," Chris answered, and Drew slowly released the breath he hadn't known he was holding. Although Chris's answer was somewhat subdued, Drew saw it as an opening, a beginning. He threw a grateful glance at Vienna, hardly able to fathom just how she had accomplished so easily what he'd been trying to achieve for the past six months. Small though it might seem, he knew they'd just made an important breakthrough—one he'd almost given up hope of ever achieving. Perhaps now, he'd be able to start knocking down the barriers Chris had erected between them. Perhaps now he could begin to get to know his son.

Vienna felt her face flush with pleasure at the look of gratitude that flashed in Drew's eyes. She quickly dropped her gaze and glanced at her watch.

"Good heavens!" she exclaimed. "I nearly forgot. I have to be at the clinic in an hour. I'm expecting a delivery this morning from a pharmaceutical company, and I have to be there to sign for the order."

"Are you a doctor?" Chris asked as he gently patted Daisy, who had moved to stand beside him.

"Yes," she replied. "But not a people doctor. I'm a vet."

"Wow!" Chris was gazing at her with renewed interest. "Do you have lots of animals at the clinic? Can I come and see where you work?"

"Actually, there are only a couple of cats in the sick bay at the moment," she told him. "But I'd love to show you around if you want to come by."

Chris turned to Drew. "Can we?" he asked.

Drew blinked, hardly able to believe that Chris was consulting him. "Fine with me," he said, and was instantly rewarded with a smile from the boy. "But first, let's pay your grandfather a visit."

"Good idea," Vienna agreed as she leaned toward Chris. She put her hand on his shoulder and spoke in a loud whisper. "You'll have to ask Tobias to tell you some stories about your dad when he was a kid." She nodded at Drew, who was watching the exchange with amused interest.

"Fair's fair," Drew said with a hint of laughter in his voice. "And I'm sure if you ask your grandfather, he'll be happy to tell you all kinds of stories about Vienna, as well," he countered.

"Did you live here, too?" Chris asked, smiling up at Vienna in obvious enjoyment of what was happening.

"She spent the summers and holidays here," Drew informed his son. "And every September when she returned to school, she'd leave behind half a dozen animals she'd found and adopted over the holidays. I usually got the job of looking after the zoo that consisted of anything from injured rabbits and abandoned kittens to wild birds. You name it, she brought it home."

"Neat-o!" Chris's wide-eyed expression told of his admiration.

"Don't you let him fool you," Vienna warned, trying to hide the warmth racing through her at the familiar teasing tone in Drew's voice. "Most of the time, your father was the one who found the animals and brought them to me to look after."

Chris turned and gazed at his father for a long moment. Vienna could almost see the boy's mind turning over what she had said. Suddenly, she found herself thinking that Chris's hostility toward Drew could well have been Natalie's doing. It was possible she'd fed the boy stories about a father who'd abandoned him. That would explain why Chris seemed unwilling to trust his father, unwilling, no doubt, to let himself be hurt.

"We'd better get going," Vienna said into the silence.

"I'll run upstairs and get my coat," Drew answered, and made his way from the room.

Vienna retrieved her heavy winter jacket from the closet and turned to find Chris staring at her. "Was that true?" the boy asked. "About my da—About him?"

"I have no reason to lie to you Chris," she said softly, and then watched helplessly as the boy's eyes filled with tears. It was all she could do not to pull him into her arms. Instead, she crouched down beside him. "I don't know what anyone else has told you about your father, but if I were you I'd try to make up my own mind about the kind of man he is. He loves you very much, Chris. You just have to give him a chance." She smiled at him. "Come on, let's wait for your dad in the car, shall we? He knows how to lock up."

Chris nodded, and blinking back his tears, he managed a tentative smile.

The drive to the hospital was completed in silence, and as Vienna brought the old station wagon to a halt in the parking lot, her apprehension mounted. With a quick glance at Drew, she noticed the tiny pulse jumping in his throat, and a jaw that was tight with tension.

As they crossed to the hospital entrance, Vienna acknowledged several greetings from passersby. Inside, the familiar smell of disinfectant filled the air. She headed for the elevators, with Drew and Chris by her side.

When they reached the fourth floor, they approached the nurses' desk, but there was no one in attendance.

Vienna turned to Drew. "Tobias's room is number three, the second one on the left," she said pointing to the hallway on her right. "If you give me a few minutes..."

"All right, but don't be too long," Drew answered.

Vienna made her way to the door, and with a brief tap, she went inside.

Tobias was lying in bed, propped up with pillows. Vienna was relieved to see that the color of his skin was much healthier than it had been during those first few days. He'd always been an active man, and at seventy-five, he still believed he could do all the things he'd done at forty. Though his dark hair was now nearly solid gray, and the lines on his face reflected the joys and sorrows of his life, he was still a very handsome man.

"Hi there, Tobias," she said in a cheerful voice. "You look good this morning."

"I feel great this morning" came the gruff reply. His eyes crinkled into a smile, and he held out his hand to her.

She immediately grasped it and sat down on the edge of the bed. Leaning forward, she kissed his cheek, feeling the roughness of his unshaven face.

"I see the nurse hasn't been in to shave you yet," she said, her tone light and teasing.

"That damned nurse couldn't shave a porcupine," Tobias mumbled. "Besides, I told her I'd do it myself today." He turned blue eyes to meet hers. "What brings you here this early?" he asked, studying her closely now.

She took a deep breath and said, "I have a surprise for you."

"A surprise? What kind of surprise?" he asked, his thick bushy eyebrows lifting questioningly.

She hesitated, unsure whether simply to blurt it out or to get to the point slowly. She opted for the latter. "Well, there's a couple of people outside who've come a long way to see you," she began.

"And who might they be?" Tobias asked. "Not more doctors to poke and prod at me, I hope."

Vienna smiled, and shook her head. "I'm not sure exactly how to tell you this...."

"Spit it out, child. Don't dilly-dally," he ordered.

"All right," Vienna said. "Drew is here. And before you say anything...he's brought Christopher, your grandson."

"Drew?" The name was barely a whisper, and for a moment Vienna saw something flicker in the depths of his eyes before it was quickly controlled.

Tobias was silent for a long moment, and Vienna had to squeeze his hand to regain his attention. He blinked at her and spoke again. "And my...*grandson*, did you say?" He stared at her incredulously. He withdrew his hands from hers and pressed one against his heart.

Fear and concern had her on her feet, but as she reached for the button to signal the nurse, Tobias stopped her.

"I'm fine, I'm fine," he assured her as he sank back against the pillows. "When you say surprise, you do mean surprise. Tell me. How old is the youngster? Where is he? I want to see him."

"Chris is seven. And they're both outside in the hallway," she told him, moving now to the door. "Shall I ask them to come in?"

Tobias frowned. "Just the boy. I just want to see the boy," was the stiff reply.

"Tobias! How can you say that?" Vienna came back toward the bed and sat down.

"Now, don't give me one of your looks," said the old man gruffly. "I washed my hands of that son of mine eight years ago, when he defied me and went off with that...that...floozy...." His face was beginning to redden.

"Stop it this minute," Vienna scolded him, surprised at how angry she felt. "If the nurse comes in and sees you like this, you'll have to stay here for another month."

Tobias took several deep, steadying breaths, and slowly his color began to return to normal. "Is she here, too?" he asked suddenly.

"No. Natalie's dead," she told him quietly. Tobias closed his eyes and said nothing.

"Listen to me, Tobias," Vienna continued, and at her words Tobias gazed at her once more. "Drew is here because I called him. During those first few hours after I found you, I thought you were going to die. I didn't know what to do. He's your son, and he had a right to know."

Tobias sighed and gently traced a finger down her cheek. "I understand why you did it, Vienna...but there's just too much water under the bridge—"

"Don't say that," she interrupted. "He's come all the way from California. The least you could do is see him, talk to him. Eight years is a long time, Tobias. Things have changed. You have a grandson to consider. And Christopher needs you," she added softly, all the while fighting the urge to shake the stubbornness out of him.

Tobias crossed his arms and stared at her. "I'll see the boy, but you can tell Drew..."

"Why don't you tell me yourself?" said a deep voice from behind them.

Vienna gasped and swung around to see Drew, arm outstretched, holding the door open, his face dark with anger. Seconds later, Christopher followed, ducking under his father's arm and coming to a halt just inside the room.

"I don't want to wait out in the hall," Christopher said, his tone bordering on defiant. "I want to see my grandfather—" He stopped when he saw the figure on the bed, and let his gaze sweep over the man lying there.

Vienna held her breath as grandfather and grandson eyed each other. Turning, she let her glance slide over the three generations of Sheridans and marveled at how alike they were—dark, proud and stubborn.

As Tobias's gaze lingered on the young boy, Vienna saw the tears welling up in the older man's eyes.

"I'm your grandfather, boy," Tobias managed at last, but his voice was husky with emotion he was trying desperately to hide. He coughed and cleared his throat, quickly regaining control. "Come here and let me have a look at you."

Christopher cast a brief glance at Vienna as he passed her. "You must be very sick, if you have to stay here," Chris commented, crossing to the bedside.

"I was very sick, but I'm feeling much better," Tobias said. "Why don't you hop up here beside me and tell me all about yourself, Chris?" Tobias patted the bedcovers.

Christopher turned and glanced first at Vienna, then at Drew, as though looking for approval or permission.

"Stay if you want to, Chris." Drew kept his eyes on the boy. "I'll wait for you outside in the hall." With that, Drew moved away from the door, letting it slide shut behind him.

Vienna quickly crossed to the door. "I'll leave the two of you to get acquainted," she said, but not before she threw an angry look at Tobias.

"You live in California, I hear," Tobias was saying, too preoccupied with Chris to even notice she was leaving.

Glancing quickly up and down the hallway, she spotted Drew standing at the end of the corridor, looking out the window. His shoulders were sagging slightly and his head was resting against the glass in a gesture of defeat and frustration.

Vienna felt her heart turn over as she realized for the first time just how difficult the decision to come home must have been for Drew. She felt partly to blame for the hurt Tobias had inflicted. After all, hadn't she been the one to call Drew?

"I should have known nothing would have changed," Drew said as she reached him.

"He just needs some time," Vienna said, though her tone was far from convincing.

Drew swung around and she heard his laughter—a mocking laughter, that made her flinch. "Time, that's a laugh. After eight years, he's still the same stubborn old fool he always was." Drew ran a hand through his thick black hair and clenched his teeth in frustration. "Why the hell did I bother to come back?" The question was spoken softly, as if to himself.

"You came back because you care about that... stubborn old fool," Vienna said.

Drew's eyes lifted to hers, and for a long moment their glances met and held. Something stirred deep inside her, sending faint little tremors racing through her. It was all she could do not to reach out and try to soothe away the pain and worry from his handsome face. His expression softened for a moment, and a smile touched the corners of his mouth—a change that sent her heart galloping madly.

"Vienna? Is that you?" The voice came from farther down the corridor, effectively breaking the spell that seemed to have woven around them.

Drew turned back to the window. Vienna, still somewhat in a daze, turned and saw Dr. Bruce McGregor—tall, blond and attractive, his white hospital coat waving in the breeze he created—bearing down on them.

"Hello, Bruce."

"What a wonderful way to start my morning," Bruce said, his handsome features breaking into a brilliant smile. He leaned forward and kissed Vienna on the cheek. "I'm not interrupting anything, am I?" he asked, glancing at Drew.

"Bruce, I don't believe you knew Drew Sheridan, Tobias's son," Vienna said.

"Pleased to meet you," Bruce said, extending his hand toward Drew. "I'm sure Vienna has told you that your father is coming along nicely?"

"Yes, thank you," Drew said politely, shaking the proffered hand.

"I'm sure your father will be happy to know you're here," Bruce went on.

"If you'll excuse me," Drew said abruptly, then strode down the hall.

Vienna frowned as she watched Drew walk away, but before she could go after him, Bruce put his arms around her and pulled her close. "We're still on for tonight, aren't we?" he asked, smiling down at her. "Now that Tobias is off the critical list, our lives can get back to normal." He kissed her nose. "I've missed you."

Over Bruce's shoulder Vienna could see Drew standing at the nurses' desk. He was too far away for her to read his expression, but somehow she sensed his disapproval. "Bruce, please... Not here," she said, surprised at the firmness of her voice.

Bruce frowned as he released his hold on her. "Sorry, darling," he said. "Did I hurt you?"

"Dr. McGregor you're wanted in emergency.

Dr. McGregor to emergency, please."

The disembodied voice of the hospital P.A. system startled them both.

"Oops... Got to go, love. I'll pick you up tonight at seven. Wear that red dress I like so much. Tonight's going to be special." With a wave of his hand, he hurried away.

Vienna let out a sigh as she watched the departing figure. She liked Bruce, liked him a lot. He was fun to be with, and for the past six months, since he'd come to work at the hospital, they'd been dating on a regular basis. But just prior to Tobias's heart attack, Bruce had begun to pressure her into a more intimate relationship. Though this hadn't surprised her, she'd found she wasn't yet ready to make that kind of commitment. So far, she'd managed to sidestep the issue, but she knew Bruce was growing impatient.

"Is something wrong?" Drew's voice cut through her thoughts and she looked up to find him gazing thoughtfully at her.

"No..." she said, trying to ignore the way her pulse had kicked into high gear at the sound of his voice.

"Maybe you could see how Chris is doing in there," Drew said, glancing at the door to his father's room. "I've decided that this whole trip was a wasted effort. I'm going to call the airport and book a flight back to San Francisco."

Chapter Three

"Don't you think that's rather a rash decision?" Vienna asked, dismayed by Drew's words.

"You heard him in there. He wants nothing to do with me," Drew countered. "He's the same stubborn fool—" He broke off. "It's his way or no way at all."

"And just what did you expect?" Vienna was suddenly angry. "Did you think he'd welcome you with open arms?"

"Of course not." It was Drew's turn to be angry.

"Then give him a chance. Give yourself a chance," she urged. "For the past eight years he hasn't heard a word from you . . . nothing. I know he told you to get out and never come back, but I saw him when you drove away with Natalie, and he was devastated. He kept telling me you'd be back. . . . He couldn't believe you'd actually go. When he said those things to you, he was angry and frustrated. He couldn't accept the fact that you were a grown man and entitled to make your own choices, your own decisions. Yes, he was stubborn. But so were you. And while he's never said it, I know he regrets what happened.''

Drew stared at her for a long moment, and strangely, he found himself admiring the fire he could see in the depths of her lovely gray eyes. She'd always been an earnest little thing, ready to fight for the underdog, which usually had taken the form of some lost or injured animal she'd found in the countryside around the fruit orchards owned by his father.

''I appreciate what you're trying to do, Vienna, but I think that this time it's a lost cause.''

''How can you say that?'' Vienna demanded. ''You haven't given it a chance. Do you know what I think? I think you're a coward. Running away was your solution eight years ago. And from what I can gather, that action only created more problems. Don't you think it's time you stayed and tried to resolve this, once and for all?''

Vienna watched in fascination as the skin across Drew's cheekbones tightened and his eyes darkened to a deadly black. When his hands came up to grasp her arms, she knew she'd gone too far, but it was much too late to retract the challenge she had issued.

He drew her toward him, and as his breath gently fanned her face, she tried to ignore the way her heart began to accelerate in response to his touch. She was aware of a heady excitement chasing along her nerve endings, and she knew her reaction had everything to do with the fact that Drew was standing close—much too close. Dear heaven, what was happening to her?

she wondered, as she tried to control emotions suddenly gone awry.

"All right, you win." Drew's tone was as chilly as the December temperature outside. "We'll stay, but only for a few days. But if I were you, I wouldn't expect miracles."

He released her and she felt weak with relief. Before she could speak, the door to Tobias's room opened and they turned to see Chris emerge.

"Gramps wants to talk to you," Chris said, his eyes on Drew.

Vienna managed to choke back her surprise and kept her face expressionless as Drew threw her a brief glance. But the fact that Chris was referring to Tobias as "Gramps" was definitely an encouraging sign. They'd obviously hit it off, she thought, as a smile curled at the corners of her mouth.

"Gramps?" Drew murmured under his breath.

"Chris, why don't you come to the clinic with me?" Vienna suggested. "When your father is through, he can meet us there."

"Neat-o!" The boy broke into a smile and turned to his father for approval.

"The clinic is on the corner of Pine Street and Cherry Lane," she went on. "I took it over from Bill Logan."

Drew nodded. "It seems I have little say in the matter," he said, a hint of irony in his tone.

Chris came to Vienna's side and put his hand in hers, and together they began to walk toward the elevators. They had taken only a few steps when Vienna stopped and looked back.

Drew was standing at the door of his father's room, his hand poised in readiness to push it open. As though sensing her eyes on him, he turned, and in that moment Vienna glimpsed such a vulnerable look on his face that her heart ached for him.

She released Chris's hand and returned to where Drew stood. "Just remember," she said softly, "it's only a battlefield if you make it one."

A fleeting smile crossed his features, and seconds later, he disappeared inside.

Throughout the short journey to the clinic, Chris asked questions about her work as a vet. Though Vienna was anxious to find out what he and Tobias had talked about, she thought it best to let the boy broach the subject first.

Once they reached the clinic, Chris was much more interested in touring the facilities. Starting with the small reception area, she gave him a guided tour, showing him the three consulting rooms, the small dispensary, the operating room, and the area used to house the pets awaiting pickup by their owners.

"This is Snow," Vienna told Chris, pointing to the beautiful long-haired white cat. "And the orange-and-white cat is called Patches. She's only six months old."

"Were they sick?" Chris asked, tentatively moving closer to the two cages, where the cats were stirring.

"Snow's owner brought her in yesterday afternoon. She'd cut her paw on a piece of barbed wire. After I cleaned and sewed up the wound, I kept her overnight just to make sure she was all right. Patches, here, looks like she's feeling a little better today, too."

"What happened to her?" Christopher wanted to know.

"Well, when owners don't want their cats to have kittens, I do a special operation. It's called spaying."

With a concerned expression on his face, Christopher carefully put his hand out toward Patches.

"Would you like to hold her?" Vienna asked.

"Yes, please" came the reply. "But will I hurt her?"

"Not if you've very gentle. She could probably use a little loving right now." Seeing Chris's wide-eyed and eager expression, she felt sure both parties would benefit.

Vienna opened the cage, and careful of the cat's stitches, she lifted Patches from the blanket. "Put one hand under her back legs like this," she instructed, showing Christopher how she was holding Patches, "and the other hand here."

Eyes wide with wonder, Christopher held Patches carefully in his arms.

"Oh, there's the delivery van. Will you be all right for a minute?" she asked.

Christopher could only nod, but the smile on his face made Vienna's heart melt.

After dealing with the delivery, Vienna returned to the "recovery room," as she dubbed it. Christopher was seated on a small stool and Patches was resting on his lap. A loud purring sound told its own story.

"She likes me," Chris informed her, his face beaming with pride. "She was licking my fingers, and her tongue is all rough."

"Their tongues are like that because they use them to comb their fur," Vienna explained.

"You sure know a lot about animals," Christopher said. "I'd like to be a vet, too, when I grow up."

"I bet you'd make a terrific vet," Vienna answered. "You could get some practice right now, if you like," she added.

"Okay. What can I do?"

"Well, if you want to bring Patches through to the examining table, I could check and see how her stitches look."

Christopher did as he was bid, and gently stroked the cat while Vienna examined her handiwork. Chris curled up his nose a little at the sight of the sutures, but Vienna pretended not to notice. Moments later, Chris began asking questions, and for the next little while, Vienna was kept busy supplying answers.

After returning Patches to her cage, Vienna gave Chris a few pet magazines to browse through. Then she placed a call to the owners of both cats, informing them they could be picked up at any time. She had only just hung up the telephone when the bell above the front door jangled, announcing someone's arrival.

It could only be Drew, thought Vienna, and her heart began to kick against her breastbone. What had Tobias said? Had they fought? Had they decided on a temporary truce?

"We're in here," Vienna called from the small office at the rear of the building. Chris glanced up from the magazine he'd been flipping through.

Drew stopped in the doorway. At the sight of the grim expression on his face, her hopes plummeted.

"How did it go?" she asked, her tone even.

"To be honest, I'm not really sure," Drew replied. "We didn't fight, if that's what you mean. But we didn't resolve anything, either." He unbuttoned his coat and glanced toward his son. "What have you been up to?"

"I was helping Vienna," Christopher told him proudly, obviously pleased that Drew had asked.

"What did you do?" Drew crossed to the old two-seater couch where his son was sitting.

"She showed me how to hold a cat, and then she looked at the cat's stitches. The cat is orange and white and she's called Patches. Her tongue felt funny, but she liked me, 'cause she was purring like mad."

Drew smiled at his son and gently ruffled the boy's hair. "Sounds like you were a great helper," he said, and at his words a smile of pleasure lit Chris's features.

"I'm going to be a vet just like Vienna when I grow up," the boy said.

"I'll take you on as my partner," Vienna said, then smiled ruefully. "If I'm still in business," she added, almost to herself.

Drew's eyes darted to meet hers, a concerned frown on his face. "I thought Bill Logan's clinic did very well."

Vienna felt her face flush under his probing gaze, and silently admonished herself for letting her guard down. "Oh, Bill's clinic did fine," she agreed, managing to smile. She refrained from adding that it was her clinic that had the problem.

Drew's frown deepened. "There's something not quite right here," he said, surprising her with his astuteness. "Want to talk about it?" He spoke in that gentle, yet persuasive, tone he'd used so often in the past.

Vienna hesitated for a moment, surprised to find that she was on the verge of confiding in him. Drew had always been a good listener, but the problems she was facing regarding the clinic were hers, and hers alone.

"It's nothing I can't handle," she stated calmly, and tried to ignore the look of disappointment that came into his eyes.

She hadn't even told Tobias about her run-in with dog breeder Olivia Harvey-Smythe, several months ago. It had been a result of that unforgettable incident that her livelihood—the clinic—was in jeopardy. Sixty percent of the pet owners in town were driving to the vet in Springfield, twenty miles away, and there wasn't a damn thing she could do about it.

Owning and running a veterinary clinic had been her dream for as long as she could remember, and she was determined that come hell or high water she'd ride out this patch of rough weather.

She glanced at Drew, who was watching her through narrowed eyes. But before he could voice the question she saw in his eyes, Chris broke the silence.

"Want to come and see the cats?" he asked.

Drew turned to his son. "Sure," he answered, and rose to follow the boy, but not before leveling her a glance that said the subject was far from closed.

Alone now, Vienna released the breath she'd been holding. She found Drew's interest and concern touching, but the fact that she'd been tempted to confide in him disturbed her greatly. Thoughtfully, she acknowledged that even in the short time since he'd arrived, she felt as if some of the burden of responsibility had been lifted from her shoulders.

Not that she wasn't used to coping with problems on her own—she'd done it all her life, and prided herself in being able to deal with anything. But Tobias's heart attack had frightened her more than she cared to admit.

Tobias was one of the few people in her life she'd been able to count on, and the thought of losing him had rocked her to the core.

Since her father's death, Tobias had stepped in and taken over his role, doing a better job than either of Vienna's own parents had done. But then, she'd always known that her arrival into her parents' lives after fifteen years of marriage had come as something of a surprise—and not a welcome one, at that.

Well-known in the field of botanical research, John and Barbara Forrester had found a child both cumbersome and inconvenient—especially in the jungle regions of South America, where they were conducting their research. Though they had taken her with them, once they'd arrived at the base camp, Vienna had been left under the care of anyone they could recruit.

She had been six years old when her mother died from a fever she'd contracted in the jungles of Brazil. Her father had been totally devastated. Unable to continue his research, he had decided to return to the States. There he'd agreed to go on a series of lecture tours, first making arrangements for Vienna to enter a private boarding school for girls in Washington State.

Vienna had spent the next three years at the boarding school, hearing from her father only occasionally and seeing him rarely. She spent her summers either at the school or at a friend's home—never with her father.

But the summer after she turned ten, John Forrester had appeared at the school to inform her that he'd arranged for them to spend the summer with an old friend of his, Tobias Sheridan, who was also her godfather.

Though Vienna had been surprised at this turn of events, anything was better than staying at the school, and so they'd made the journey to Peachville, in the fruit-growing Okanagan Valley of British Columbia. She had immediately fallen in love—not only with the region and its beautiful lakes and abundant fruit trees, but with the small town itself.

Her father had stayed for two short weeks, and in that time Vienna realized that he still hadn't come to terms with the death of her mother. Only in his work did he find any solace, and so, leaving her in Tobias's care, he'd returned to South America and the jungles he and his wife had loved so dearly.

At the end of that summer, Vienna had returned to the boarding school. A few months later, she'd been summoned to the office and told of her father's death.

She'd accepted the news calmly, but had been inwardly ashamed that she felt nothing—no sense of loss, no grief. It wasn't until a week later, when Tobias had arrived to offer her a home with him, that she'd broken down and cried.

She'd known even then that she wanted to become a vet, and known, too, that in order to gain entrance to a veterinary college, she would need exceptional grades. Strangely, she'd found it easy to tell Tobias her plan to stay on at the school and complete her education.

Tobias had insisted that she return to Peachville each summer and for holidays, and it was there she'd spent some of the happiest times of her life. Through those long days she'd helped Drew and Tobias harvest the fruit in the orchards, and had spent every spare minute helping Bill Logan in his veterinary clinic in town.

Without Tobias's love and support, Vienna doubted she would have achieved her goal of becoming a vet. Drew, too, had encouraged her, and though he was six years her senior, he'd always made her feel part of the family, accepting her presence without resentment. He'd teased and tormented her the way a brother would a sister, and they'd formed a friendship she'd secretly treasured.

Tobias meant the world to her, and the fact that he was indeed recovering from the heart attack was all that mattered at the moment. She'd contacted Drew out of panic and fear, but now that he was here, she by no means regretted her decision.

It would take a while for Tobias and Drew to resolve their differences. Eight years was a long time.

But Christopher's presence would, she felt sure, go a long way toward helping to bridge the gap.

A sudden flurry of noise from the outer office effectively brought Vienna from her reverie. She rose and hurried to the door.

Chapter Four

Vienna came to an abrupt halt at the sight of Sam Williamson, a local house builder, carrying a beautiful golden retriever in his arms. There was a deep gash in the dog's left hind leg, and its coat was sticky with blood that was still oozing from the open wound.

"Vienna! There you are," Sam said, relief evident in his tone. "I found this poor fellow lying by the side of the old road that leads into town."

"Bring him in here, Sam," Vienna instructed, crossing to open the door to the small operating room.

"Is he going to die?" The question came from Chris, whose voice was a whisper of emotion.

Vienna glanced in Chris's direction. Pressed up against his father, his face was white and his eyes were wide with fear.

Vienna held his gaze. "No, Chris, he won't die," she told him calmly. "He's got a pretty bad gash, though, and it will have to be dealt with. Thanks, Sam," she said as he stepped back from the table, making room for her.

The dog tried to lift his head, but feebly sank down again. Then he began to whine softly.

"I can't stay, I'm late already," Sam told her, adjusting the cap on his head. "I took the old road because it's a shortcut for me. But when I spotted him lying there... well, I just couldn't leave him," he said as he moved toward the door.

"Thanks for all you've done, Sam," Vienna said, bending over the dog's prone figure, quickly assessing his condition. "I'll let you know how he makes out," she added as he left.

The dog was in shock and his vital signs showed that he needed to be stabilized. With gentle fingers, she determined that there were no other injuries. He was a young dog—less than a year old. She guessed that he'd met up with a wild cat, or perhaps had disturbed a sleepy bear and been sideswiped for his inquisitiveness.

She knew Drew and Chris were watching her intently but she ignored them, and it was several minutes before she raised her head and adjusted the intravenous drip she'd inserted. When she'd finished, she stroked the dog's head. "Good boy. We'll have you fixed up in no time," she said softly.

"Will he really be all right?" Chris asked, taking a step away from his father and moving toward the table.

Vienna turned to him and smiled. "He'll be fine," she assured him. "But before I can close the wound, I have to call the owner."

"Why?" Chris wanted to know, inching toward the dog's head.

"Well, just like a doctor who needs permission to operate on a patient, I need the owner's permission to do what's necessary for the dog," she explained.

"Is it all right if I pet him?" the boy asked, his hand reaching tentatively toward the animal.

Vienna hesitated. "I don't . . ." she began, but the pleading look in Christopher's eyes stopped her. "All right. Tell you what. You can keep an eye on him for me while I call the owner. But don't touch anything," she cautioned.

"I won't," Chris promised solemnly.

Vienna smiled and gently ruffled his hair with her hand. "I'll go make that call."

Turning, she found herself face-to-face with Drew. As their glances collided, she saw a look of admiration in the depths of his dark eyes and was surprised at the feeling of pleasure that suddenly spread through her.

Drew took a step back to let her pass. "You know who he belongs to, then?" he said.

Vienna crossed to her office. "I'm pretty sure he's from Hillcrest Kennels," she said, moving to her desk. She sat down and reached for the telephone. Her hand hovered over the receiver for a moment, then with a sigh she withdrew it.

"Is something wrong?" Drew asked from the doorway.

Vienna shot him a glance and felt her face grow warm under his questioning stare. She reached for the telephone again and this time she dialed the number, careful to avoid Drew's gaze. "It's just that I hate being the bearer of bad news," she told him, annoyed with herself for not doing a better job of hiding the anxiety she was feeling at having to contact Olivia Harvey-Smythe.

As she listened to the phone ringing, she picked up a pencil from the desk and began to doodle nervously on the blotting pad. She could feel Drew's eyes on her and studiously she avoided looking at him.

"Hillcrest Kennels." Olivia Harvey-Smythe's voice rang in her ear and abruptly brought Vienna back to the task in hand.

"Mrs. Harvey-Smythe? Vienna Forrester calling."

There was silence for a moment. "What do you want?" the harsh voice on the other end demanded.

"I'm sorry to bother you," Vienna began evenly, determined to hold on to her temper.

"Get on with it," came the crisp reply.

Vienna tightened her grip on the receiver and continued. "A male golden retriever has been brought into my clinic. He was found on the old road into town on the north end of your property. He's approximately ten months old, and he has a deep cut on his left hind leg—"

"Don't touch him! I'll be right there." The words were practically shouted at her, causing Vienna to pull the phone away from her ear.

Before Vienna could say more, the line went dead. Stunned, she stared at the receiver for several seconds. Anger surged through her and she had to take several deep, steadying breaths before putting the phone down. Mumbling to herself, she ran a hand through her short curls. Glancing up, she found Drew's dark eyes watching her intently.

She quickly controlled her features and rose from the chair. She crossed to the door, her intention being to check on the injured dog once more, but Drew's hand came out to bar her way.

"What was that all about?" he asked, the deep, rich tones of his voice adding a new dimension to the tension tightening inside her.

"Nothing," she said, and tried to push his arm aside. It was like trying to move a mountain. Her hand dropped away and she turned to meet his penetrating gaze.

"Sounded like a lot more than that," he commented dryly.

Vienna bit back a sigh and let her glance slide past the strong column of Drew's throat, over the blue sweater that covered the broad expanse of his chest. Her head would fit nicely against his shoulder, she thought distractedly; and for a fleeting moment she was tempted to give in to the overpowering need to be held, to be comforted.

She felt herself sway toward him and hastily, she pulled back, just in time. Gathering her scattered wits, she blinked rapidly, and taking a step back, she broke the invisible threads that seemed to have wrapped themselves around her body and her emotions.

"Nothing I can't handle," she told him, thankful to find her voice as well as her composure. "Excuse me, but I'd like to check on the dog again."

Bravely, she brought her eyes back to his, and when she saw his expression, her breath caught in her throat.

Drew opened his mouth to speak but at the sound of the outer door opening, he turned instead to see the newcomers.

"Vienna! It's only us."

"Hello, Sara. Hi, Tim," said Vienna, more than a little relieved at the interruption. She moved past Drew to greet her friend and part-time receptionist at the clinic, Sara Boyd.

"Sorry, I didn't know you were busy," Sara said, flashing a smile at Drew.

"Sara, I'd like you to meet Drew Sheridan, Tobias's son," Vienna said. "Drew, this is Sara and her son, Tim. They live in the flat upstairs, and Sara helps me in the clinic."

"Nice to meet you," Drew said, stepping forward and shaking first Sara's hand, then Tim's.

"And this is Drew's son, Chris," Vienna continued, turning to Chris, who had obviously heard the commotion and had come to investigate.

"Hello, Chris," said Sara, then turned to her son. "Say hello to Chris, Tim."

"Hi," said Tim.

"Hi."

The boys eyed each other for a moment before Chris shyly retreated into the operating room. Tim hesitated, then followed.

Sara's glance slid back to Vienna. "We popped in to see if you wanted to come to the mall with us and have lunch," she said. "There's no school this afternoon, thanks to a teachers' meeting. Tim wants to pay Santa a visit before the line gets too long."

"I'd love to come with you, but I can't," said Vienna. "Sam Williamson found one of Mrs Harvey-Smythe's retrievers lying on the road this morning."

"Not again," said Sara. "Why doesn't that woman get someone to fix the fences on the dog runs? Is he badly hurt?"

"No, thank goodness," answered Vienna. "I just called her and she's on her way."

"Do you want me to stay?" Sara asked, a look of concern on her face.

"No, it's all right, I'll manage," said Vienna. "I wouldn't want Tim to miss out on his visit to Santa. Besides, it's your day off, remember?"

"Mom?" Tim reappeared tugging at his mother's sleeve. "Can Chris come with us to the mall to see Santa?" he asked. "He's from California and he says he's been to Disneyland twice." Tim's tone was full of envy.

"Sure . . . if it's all right with his father," Sara told him, as she glanced toward Drew.

"Would you like to go, Chris?" Drew asked his son, who stood in the doorway.

Chris nodded, his eyes sparkling with eagerness. The boys had quickly broken through the barrier of shyness and had obviously hit it off. Vienna was glad. During the brief time she'd spent with Chris, she'd sensed he was both confused and a trifle lonely. Making friends with someone his own age would, she felt sure, be good for him.

"Then it's fine with me," Drew said, following his words with a smile.

"You're welcome to join us, too, of course," Sara added.

"Thank you. But I'll stay and see if I can't be of some help here. You don't mind if I hang around, do you, Vienna?" he asked.

"No..." she replied, surprised that he'd opted to stay.

"Let's go, boys. We'll be back in about an hour." The door closed behind them.

Vienna turned to Drew. "You don't have to stay."

"True," he acknowledged. "But the boys seemed to be getting along so well, I just thought they'd feel less inhibited if I wasn't around."

There was no faulting his logic, Vienna thought. And as she moved toward the operating room, she felt both relieved and grateful that she wouldn't be alone when Olivia Harvey-Smythe arrived.

Vienna checked the dog's condition once more, pleased to note that his vital signs had stabilized. As she gently stroked the animal's silky head, she found herself wishing she didn't have to wait for Olivia Harvey-Smythe's permission to do what she'd been trained to do.

It had taken time for her to come to terms with the fact that a veterinary practice was also a business. To Vienna's way of thinking, the knowledge, skills and expertise she'd acquired at veterinary college were to be used to help an ill or injured animal, regardless of what the cost might be.

But she had quickly come to realize that a vet who lived by that philosophy would soon be a vet without a practice. Not that she hadn't done her share of "freebies"; but the practical side of her nature had convinced the emotional side to keep those cases to a minimum.

Vienna turned to find Drew staring at her. She felt her pulse kick into high gear and wondered—not for the first time since his arrival—why she should find his gaze quite so disconcerting.

Though she hadn't seen him in eight years, he was still by far the most handsome man she'd ever known. But now she was aware of a harshness in his face and a cynicism in his eyes that she found troubling.

That he was a man familiar with success was evident in the aura of confidence and power that seemed to radiate from him, but the warmth, tenderness and laughter that had once been an integral part of Drew were missing.

Fleetingly, she recalled the pain and vulnerability she'd glimpsed when he'd told her about Chris's unexpected arrival in his life. She instinctively knew that hidden somewhere beneath the cool facade he showed to the world was the man she'd once known, the man she'd once thought herself in love with.

"Correct me if I'm wrong," Drew said, effectively cutting through her wayward thoughts, "but I get the distinct impression that you're not looking forward to the upcoming meeting with our injured friend's owner."

He was right, of course. There was little point denying it. Yet, as she crossed to the doorway once again, Vienna found she was unwilling to burden Drew with her problems. "Let me just say that Mrs. Harvey-Smythe is not my favorite person, and that the feeling is mutual."

Drew shifted his body just enough to block her way. His dark eyes examined her face with a thoroughness that sent her pulse thundering in her ears.

"Nice try," said Drew. "But there's more to it than that. Come on, Vienna. Talk to me. You used to say I was a good listener. Why don't you tell me what this is all about?"

Emotion suddenly caught in Vienna's throat, making it impossible for her to speak. Drew's comment that he'd always been a good listener brought all kinds of forgotten memories to the forefront of her mind.

How well she remembered the times during those summers so long ago that they'd sat and talked. At least, *she*'d talked, telling Drew all her hopes and dreams about becoming a vet.

Vienna sighed and met his gaze. "I never could put one over on you, could I?" she admitted, a hint of nostalgia in her tone now.

"Never" was his quiet reply.

"Well..." Vienna began. "Mrs. Olivia Harvey-Smythe runs a kennel on the outskirts of town. She moved to Peachville about a year ago and she's a champion breeder of golden retrievers. She has quite a reputation in breeding circles, and her dogs have won countless championships.

"Retrievers, however, are a breed that likes to roam. As Sara said, the dog runs at Hillcrest are in need of repair, but that's not a priority with the owner. Every now and then, one of her dogs manages to find a hole in the fence. They are, by nature, hunting dogs. Their instincts are strong, and when they're let loose, they have a tendency to head for the hills. They usually come back, of course—sometimes on the same day, sometimes several days later.'' She glanced at him to find his eyes intent on her.

"Go on," urged Drew.

"Last September, Brigadoon, one of her prize show dogs, dug an escape route under the fence and off he went. He was gone for a couple of days, but as I said, that wasn't unusual." Vienna swallowed at the memory of that awful afternoon when they'd brought a torn and bloodied Brigadoon to the clinic.

Drew's hands came up to gently clasp her shoulders, and she found his touch infinitely comforting.

"A farmer found Brig in one of his fields," Vienna went on. "He was miles from home, and how he'd managed to drag himself there, no one knows." A shiver chased down her spine.

"What had happened to him?" Drew asked softly.

She was silent for a long moment. "He'd been mauled by a bear," she said at last. "At least, that's the only explanation we could think of, considering the injuries he had. He'd probably come between the bear and her cubs. He was a terrible mess." Her hands came up to her eyes as an image of Brig came sharply into focus.

Drew's hands immediately captured hers. Easing them away from her face, he clasped them tightly. His warmth and strength seemed to seep into her, effectively banishing the image from her mind.

"And..." Drew prompted gently.

Vienna blinked away tears she hadn't known were there, and continued. "Well, the farmer brought him to the clinic—but there was nothing I could do... nothing." She swallowed convulsively, recalling the feeling of helplessness that had enveloped her then. "All I could do was hold him in my arms until he slipped away."

"What was wrong with that?"

"The farmer had recognized the dog as belonging to Olivia. He'd called her and told her he was bringing Brig here. By the time Olivia arrived, it was too late—he was gone." She was silent for a long moment. "When Olivia arrived and saw Brig, she started ranting and raving. She was absolutely furious."

"But why, for heaven's sake?" Drew asked in a disbelieving tone.

"She told me that I should have done something...that I could have saved him...that I was incompetent." Vienna stopped. Tugging her hands free of Drew's, she moved past him into the reception area.

"You can't be serious," Drew said, following her.

"Oh, I'm very serious," Vienna assured him, a trace of irony in her voice. "Needless to say, she now drives twenty miles to the vet in the next town and avoids me like the plague." She refrained from adding that Olivia Harvey-Smythe's parting words that day had been bitter and resentful. She'd promised Vienna that she'd see to it that no one in town brought their animals to her clinic.

At first, Vienna hadn't taken the threat seriously, rationalizing that the woman had every right to be upset after losing one of her championship dogs. But during the past four months, business had indeed dropped off dramatically, creating a problem Vienna didn't know how to resolve.

"From what you've just told me, it's no great loss," Drew commented.

Vienna shrugged off her morose thoughts. "At least this time I can save the dog," she said, relief evident in her tone. "All his wound requires are stitches— quite a few, in fact. The only thing I am concerned about—"

But Vienna got no further, for at that moment the outer door burst open, and in came Olivia Harvey-Smythe.

"Where's my dog? Where's Ragland?" she demanded.

Chapter Five

Vienna tensed at the sound of Olivia's voice. She turned to the woman who'd joined them and was immediately conscious of her tall imposing figure—and the hostility emanating from her.

"Easy," Drew cautioned, his voice a whisper only Vienna could hear. Instantly, the tension inside her eased a little. It was enough to know he was there, and on her side.

"Well, where is he?" Olivia demanded once more, her eyes on Vienna, ignoring the man behind her.

"He's through there." Vienna pointed to the room where Ragland was lying. "His condition is stable at the moment, but the wound to his leg is deep and needs to be sutured."

"I want to see him," came the crisp reply.

The words were a command, not a request, and Vienna bit back an angry retort. "Certainly," she answered, and with a calmness she was far from feeling, she crossed to the doorway.

Vienna stood aside to let Olivia enter, then followed with a fleeting glance at Drew, who had kept silent throughout.

Olivia advanced toward the table where the dog lay and studied the animal's injured leg for what seemed an eternity. As if sensing his owner's presence, Ragland lifted his head a little to look at his mistress, a pleading expression in his deep brown eyes. But Olivia made no move to either pat or comfort him, and it was Vienna who reached out and gently stroked the dog's head.

As she soothed the animal, Vienna heard Olivia mutter under her breath before turning and striding from the room.

"He'll be permanently scarred, won't he?" she said without preamble once they were back in the reception area.

"I'm afraid so," Vienna acknowledged. "But there's no damage to his tendons, and as he's a young dog, he'll regain his strength and in time have full use of his leg."

"I want him put to sleep," announced Olivia, in a voice that was void of emotion.

Stunned, Vienna could only stare in wide-eyed astonishment. "You can't be serious!" She'd just said the dog was young and healthy and would recover. What on earth was the woman thinking?

Instinctively, Vienna turned to Drew. On his face was a reflection of the shock and anger she felt.

"Of course I'm serious." Olivia flung the words at her. "The dog's no use to either me or my kennels if he has the slightest imperfection," she went on, drawing herself up to her full height. "And you've just confirmed that he'll be permanently scarred. I can't show him in that condition."

"He'll be scarred, yes," Vienna acknowledged. "But surely he could still be useful for breeding purposes," she argued, unable to believe the woman was serious.

"That's not a consideration," came the swift reply. "He was the runt of the litter and he hasn't developed as well as I'd hoped." Olivia paused. "I don't see that this is any of your business. I've given you my instructions. Just do as I ask, and send me the bill." She turned to leave.

"Just a minute," Vienna ordered, her anger finally bursting forth. "Four months ago, you gave me a dressing down for doing nothing to save one of your prize dogs. And now you're telling me to put a perfectly sound animal to sleep." She stopped and drew a ragged breath. "I couldn't do anything for Brig, but this dog's wounds are repairable, and I refuse to destroy an animal who has more than a good chance of living a full life. I'm sorry, but I can't do as you ask."

Olivia bristled. "Then I'll simply take him to another vet who will comply with my wishes," she stated, her blue eyes flashing angrily.

"Ladies!" Drew spoke the word with authority, and both women turned to him, surprised by the intrusion. "I'm sure this matter can be cleared up without taking such drastic measures."

"Who are you?" Olivia asked, anger still evident in her voice.

"Drew Sheridan," he told her. "And you must be Olivia Harvey-Smythe, champion dog breeder. Am I right?" He followed his words with a devastating smile.

"Yes...but..." Olivia looked slightly flustered under Drew's warm, interested gaze.

"I've heard so much about you." Drew came forward to shake her hand. "I know this must be very distressing," he added in a sympathetic voice.

It was instantly obvious from the look of gratitude on Olivia's face that Drew's words had a soothing effect. The antagonism so evident moments ago seemed to magically melt away.

"Making a decision of this nature is never easy," Olivia said, a tinge of regret in her tone. "But I have a business to run, and of course my kennel's reputation is at stake. I simply can't afford to let my emotions cloud my judgment."

Vienna almost choked at this, recalling how cold and unemotional this woman had been as she studied the dog's injury. She opened her mouth to protest, but Drew flashed her a warning glance. Frowning, Vienna suppressed her angry words, silently hoping Drew knew what he was doing.

"I see your point," he said evenly. "But I wonder if there isn't a viable alternative. It does seem a shame to put the poor animal down."

"Well...perhaps you're right," Olivia conceded, somewhat reluctantly. "But you must understand," she hurried on, as though anxious to defend her actions, "I'm under a great deal of pressure at the moment. I'm leaving tomorrow for a major show back east, and just this morning two of my staff gave notice. And now this—" she waved her hand in the air for effect "—is just one more complication I don't need."

"I quite understand," Drew replied, his deep voice so full of sympathy and understanding that Vienna had to grit her teeth to stop herself from speaking out. "It's just occurred to me," Drew went on, "that rather than putting the dog to sleep, someone might enjoy him as a pet."

"That's a wonderful idea!" Vienna jumped in eagerly, unable to contain herself any longer. "I'm sure I could find someone who'd be willing to give him a good home." She threw a grateful look at Drew. It was the perfect solution, and she wished she'd thought of it. But would Olivia agree?

"Well...I'm not sure..." Olivia began uncertainly.

"It would be a generous and humane gesture," Drew pointed out casually. "But, of course, you must do what you think best."

Vienna held her breath and said a silent prayer as she watched a look of indecision cross Olivia's features.

"It *is* worth considering, I suppose," Olivia admitted at last.

"Then you agree?" Drew asked, his gaze steady.

"If a good home can be found..."

"That shouldn't be a problem, should it, Vienna?" Drew turned to her.

"No problem at all," Vienna replied, knowing that she'd keep the animal herself if she couldn't find a home for him. "I will require your signature on a release form, though," she added, and at Drew's nod she hurried toward her office.

Vienna couldn't help smiling to herself as she opened the filing cabinet and located the form. Drew's intervention had turned the whole situation around.

Perhaps if she'd been less emotional and had kept her anger in check, she might have thought of the solution herself. But, on reflection, she knew that if she had been the one to put forth the suggestion, Olivia would never have agreed to it.

Vienna knew she would be eternally grateful to Drew for what he had done. He deserved every ounce of credit—not only for coming up with the idea, but for managing to persuade Olivia to agree to it.

With the form and a pen in her hand, Vienna returned to the reception area. She held them out to Drew, then stood back and watched in silence as Olivia signed her name.

Even the fact that Olivia seemed intent on ignoring her now did nothing to dampen Vienna's feeling of joy.

"You've been so kind, so understanding," Olivia told Drew, as he walked her to the door.

"Don't mention it. Safe journey, and good luck, though I'm sure you won't need it," he added with a smile.

The moment Drew closed the door, Vienna let out a whoop of joy and did what she'd done years ago whenever Drew had done something nice for her—she threw herself into his arms.

"Oh, Drew! I don't know how to thank you." She hugged him fiercely. "You were wonderful!"

Vienna felt his body stiffen against hers and immediately the feelings of joy running rampant through her fizzled and died. She drew away to look up at his face. The harsh intensity of his gaze was decidedly unsettling and when she saw a flash of heat ignite his dark eyes, her heart began to flutter madly against her breast.

Awareness, as glorious as it was unwelcome, suddenly flared to life within her, carrying new and conflicting messages to her brain. For a fleeting moment she thought he was going to kiss her, and she closed her eyes in wondrous anticipation.

But they flew open again when his hands grasped her shoulders and he thrust her away from him. His face looked like a thundercloud, and Vienna had to bite down on the inner softness of her mouth to stop herself from crying out.

"You always were an impulsive creature," Drew said, and Vienna felt a pain wrench her heart.

"Maybe you should try it sometime," she said, turning her back on him, annoyed with herself for her foolish reaction and wanting only to hide the pain still echoing through her.

"In my experience, acting on impulse has only brought disaster," he said. At his bitter words, Vienna glanced over her shoulder at him.

His expression was unreadable, but for one heart-stopping moment she saw vulnerability and pain in his eyes. She knew instinctively that he was referring to his impulsive marriage to Natalie, and suddenly she realized that the wounds Natalie had inflicted were still raw and bleeding.

He was a man in need of comfort, perhaps even in need of love, and Vienna felt her anger and pain give way to another emotion not so easily defined.

Suddenly the door opened and Chris came hurrying in. Behind him was Sara.

"Is he all right?" Chris asked anxiously.

Before Vienna could answer, Sara spoke. "As you can tell, Chris was worried about the dog, so we brought him back. How did it go with Olivia?"

"Not bad," Vienna said, faintly relieved to switch her thoughts away from Drew.

"You have to be joking." Sara's tone was disbelieving.

"Actually, she was very cooperative," Vienna replied, with a brief glance at Drew.

A car horn blared and Sara grimaced. "That's Tim, the little monkey," she said. "I told him we'd stop at the Christmas-tree lot and pick up a tree for my mother. I'd better go. You can tell me about Olivia's visit tomorrow."

"Thanks for taking Chris to lunch," Drew said.

"No problem." With a wave, Sara was gone.

Drew turned to his son. "How was lunch? Did you see Santa?"

"Lunch was okay," the boy replied, "but we couldn't get near Santa. It was too crowded."

"Maybe you and I can try again another day," Drew suggested.

"Okay," Chris replied. Then he turned to Vienna. "Can I go in and see him?" he asked, glancing toward the open door of the operating room.

"Yes, but only for a minute. His name, by the way, is Ragland."

Vienna followed Chris, who crossed quickly to where the dog lay and began to stroke the animal's head. Ragland gave a soft, whimpering sound and tried to lick Chris's hand.

"Ragland! That's a funny name." Chris smiled at the dog as he spoke.

"What about shortening it to Rags?" Drew suggested from his vantage point just inside the door.

Chris grinned up at his father. "Yeah! Rags... That's pretty neat, Dad!"

Watching the brief exchange, Vienna saw a look of pleasure suddenly soften the harsh lines around Drew's eyes and mouth, and she felt glad.

"When will Rags be able to go home?" Chris asked.

Vienna hesitated for a moment before replying. "Actually, the owner doesn't want to keep Rags anymore. She signed him over to me."

"You mean he's your dog now?" Chris's blue eyes were wide with surprise and envy.

"Temporarily," Vienna told him. "She asked me to find him a new home."

Chris's head swiveled in his father's direction, but before he could speak, Drew held up his hand and shook his head.

"The answer is no, Chris," said Drew in a voice that brooked no argument.

Chris's shoulders slumped, and the eager expression on his features crumbled. Vienna's heart ached at the sight of the boy's dejection.

"You can help me look after Rags until I find him a new home," Vienna suggested, trying to take the edge off Chris's disappointment.

"Then I hope you don't find him a home," Chris said, darting an angry look at his father.

"That's enough, Chris. Come on, we'd better get out of Vienna's way. She has work to do," Drew said.

"Why don't you get your dad to show you where he used to go tobogganing when he was a kid. It's supposed to snow in the next day or so, remember?" Vienna was rewarded by a flicker of interest in Chris's eyes.

"When will you be finished?" Drew asked.

"In about an hour. I'll see you both later," she said cheerfully.

Chris gave Rags a long, lingering look before slowly following his father from the room.

It was three-thirty when Vienna finished scrubbing down the table where Rags had lain. She'd wheeled him into the recovery room a short time ago and at the moment he was peacefully sleeping off the effects of the anesthetic.

Before she'd administered the anesthetic, however, she'd called the Harvey-Smythe Kennels and confirmed with an assistant that the dogs were fed every evening at six o'clock and that Rags had not eaten since then.

She'd had to clip and shave a portion of Rags's beautiful coat, but in the end he'd needed only a dozen stitches to close the wound.

Vienna dropped the instruments she'd used into the sterilizer and smiled when she heard a car door slam outside.

"Are you finished? Is Rags all right?" Chris asked the moment he entered.

"He's doing fine," Vienna told him, smiling down at his eager face. "Go take a look for yourself. He's with the cats in the recovery room, probably trying to wake up."

Chris spun around and quickly disappeared from sight. Then Drew was in the doorway, and Vienna's heart began to hop and skip like a lamb in a field of clover.

"Ready to go?" he asked.

"In a minute," Vienna said and letting her gaze drop from his, she turned to follow Chris. Silently she reminded herself that she wasn't a teenager any longer, and the feelings she'd once had for Drew were a thing of the past. Eight years ago when he'd left with Natalie, she'd had to face reality and banish her hopes and dreams to a secret corner of her heart.

She'd grown up a lot since then—she'd had to. And while Drew's presence might have awakened old memories, it wouldn't do to start dreaming again. Besides, Drew and Chris would be heading back to California in the not-too-distant future. Until then, all she could hope for was that they would stay long enough to allow Tobias to form a relationship with his grandson, and perhaps, with a little luck, reestablish ties with Drew. But the three Sheridan men were proud and stubborn, and Vienna hoped she wasn't wishing for the moon.

In the recovery room, Chris sat on the floor near Rags, who lay on a blanket in one of the larger cages. Above him, the two cats in separate cages were restlessly pacing their confined areas.

"I think he remembers me," Chris said, looking up at Vienna.

"I'm sure he does," Vienna acknowledged.

"See, he's wagging his tail," Chris pointed out, his voice thick with emotion.

Vienna crouched beside him, noticing that Chris's eyes had filled with tears.

"He's going to be fine," Vienna assured him, covering his hand with hers. "He'll sleep most of the night."

"But shouldn't somebody stay with him?" Chris asked.

"Sara and Tim live upstairs. I've left a note for Sara. She'll check on Rags later when she gets home," she replied. "If there's any problem, she'll call me at home. But I don't think we need to worry. Rags won't feel like doing much."

"Won't he try to get up?" the boy persisted.

"He might," she conceded. "But I doubt he'll bother. He's had a rather traumatic day, and I think he's smart enough to know that the best thing for him is to lie quietly. Don't you, boy?" She stroked the dog's velvety ears, and Rags began to wag his tail.

Vienna's tone and Rags's response seemed to reassure Chris, but it was still with some reluctance that he got up.

Taking his small hand in hers, she turned to find Drew standing in the doorway.

"I'd say you've had a trying day, too. You look a little tired," he told her in a surprisingly gentle voice. At his words, Vienna felt a shiver chase across her nerve endings. "Let's go home," he added, the gruffness back now, making Vienna wonder if she'd merely imagined the gentleness a moment ago.

But she didn't protest when Drew opened the passenger door for her. She sank back in the seat and sighed, realizing for the first time just how tired she really was.

She hadn't had a good night's sleep since the afternoon she'd come home and found Tobias lying on the floor. How well she remembered the wait for the ambulance, the fear and anxiety she'd had to control while she performed rudimentary first aid.

Once the attendants had arrived and taken over, she couldn't recall much of what took place until they reached the hospital. They'd wheeled Tobias away, leaving her feeling more alone than ever before in her life. Even when one of the doctors appeared to tell her Tobias was holding his own, she'd felt numbed by the thought that she could have lost him.

It was early the next morning, after she'd been allowed to see Tobias, that the nurses suggested she go home and get some rest. But she'd been too frightened and too worried about Tobias to even think about leaving. She'd sat by his bedside most of the day, watching and waiting for him to open his eyes. He had, but only briefly, and his look of pain and fear had merely compounded her own anxieties.

Some hours later, she'd consented to let someone drive her home. But the house had seemed unbearably empty, and exhausted as she was, she couldn't sleep. The dogs, sensitive to her moods and emotions, had been unusually subdued, instinctively knowing that something was amiss. She couldn't remember ever before experiencing that depth of loneliness or emptiness—not even when she'd learned of her father's death.

Tobias had been the only person who'd genuinely cared for her. Tobias and Drew, she amended. And it had been at that moment, as thoughts of happier times with Tobias and Drew drifted into her mind, that she'd made the decision to contact Drew.

It was a decision she didn't regret. She glanced now at the man beside her, her gaze lingering on his handsome profile, the proud thrust of his chin, his straight nose, dark eyebrows, and long black eyelashes that any woman would envy. His lips were full and invitingly sensual, and suddenly Vienna found herself wondering what it would feel like to have them pressed firmly against hers.

At this thought, her pulse tripped over itself in surprise. As if aware of her scrutiny, Drew darted a questioning look in her direction. As his dark blue eyes collided with hers, Vienna felt her whole body react to the startling impact.

Hastily, she glanced away and focused her attention on the road ahead, trying to slow the wild hammering of her heart against her ribs.

Drew brought the car to a halt beside the house, and Vienna quickly opened the door and climbed out. The biting December wind swirled around her as she made her way toward the door leading into the kitchen.

The dogs were already barking a welcome, and soon Vienna was being greeted by Daisy and Buffy. "Good girls. Good dogs," she said as she patted and fussed with them.

Chris and Drew joined her in the kitchen and the two dogs began pushing and jostling against Chris, making him laugh at their antics.

"Can I take the dogs outside and play for a while?" Chris asked.

"Absolutely," Vienna said with a smile. "They could use a good romp."

Chris beamed back at her and in minutes they were gone.

She turned to Drew. "Oh, I forgot to mention that you'd be on your own for dinner tonight.... I hope you don't mind."

Drew studied her for a long moment and she felt her face grow warm under his gaze. "You have a date with the doctor, I presume," he remarked, and Vienna wondered at the note of disapproval in his voice.

"That's right," she said, trying to instill some cheerfulness into her answer. She felt drained and more than a little tired. As she slid off her jacket and hung it up, she found herself wishing she didn't have to go out. "I think I'll give the hospital a call," she said, her thoughts switching to Tobias now.

"I'll do that," Drew offered. "Why don't you rest up for a while? You've had an eventful afternoon."

Her heart suddenly skipped a beat at the thought that he was concerned about her. "Thanks, I think I will go and lie down."

"If the good doctor is picking you up in his car," Drew continued, "perhaps I can borrow yours so Chris and I can drop by the hospital and visit Tobias."

"Of course. Be my guest," said Vienna.

As she climbed the stairs, she found herself wondering why she wished she was going with Drew and Chris to visit Tobias, instead of spending the evening with Bruce.

Chapter Six

"Vienna." The soft tones of Drew's deep masculine voice in her ear made Vienna smile sleepily. "Vienna, wake up." His tone was more urgent now, and this time she felt a hand gently shake her shoulder. She opened her eyes to see Drew in shirt sleeves, his face only inches away.

"Drew...I'm sorry. I must have fallen asleep," she mumbled, as she struggled to sit up. The bedcovers slid away to reveal her neck and shoulders and the thin straps of the pale pink camisole she was wearing. She heard Drew's sharp intake of breath, and the muttered curse as he rose and quickly moved away from the bed.

Vienna glanced down, and with trembling fingers she pulled the covers up around her chin, feeling her face grow warm with embarrassment.

Drew came to a halt in the doorway, and Vienna noticed the tension in the corded muscles of his broad back. "Your date called. He'll be here in about forty-five minutes," he said without turning around. "I thought I'd better wake you."

"Thank you," she managed, but the door had already closed behind him.

Vienna drew a steadying breath and waited for her heart to slow its frantic pace. She hadn't expected to fall asleep, nor had she expected Drew to come and awaken her. She'd simply assumed, when she heard him call her name, that it was part of the dream she'd been having.

Annoyed at herself, she pushed the bedcovers aside. Grabbing her robe from the chair by the bed, she headed for the bathroom.

Five minutes later, she lowered herself into the warm, welcoming water. As she relaxed amid the scented bubbles, she tried to focus her thoughts on Bruce and the evening ahead. But when she closed her eyes, it was Drew's dark, brooding image that came instantly to mind.

"Damn!" she muttered, wondering not for the first time, what it was about him that so easily stirred her emotions, creating a tension deep within her.

He hadn't always affected her that way. That first summer her father brought her to Peachville, she'd formed a tentative friendship with Drew and over the years it had grown and strengthened.

Not until the evening of her sixteenth birthday did her feelings of friendship suddenly change to something else.

Her birthday was two weeks before Christmas. Ever since she'd started coming to Peachville to spend her holidays with Tobias, he'd made it a point to take her out for a special birthday dinner. Usually Drew accompanied them, but that year, he'd had other plans. She remembered feeling disappointed at the time, but Tobias had taken her to a new and rather exclusive restaurant in town, and sitting across the table from him she'd felt grown-up and very sophisticated.

They'd had a wonderful evening and when they returned home, she'd hugged and kissed her godfather, thanking him for a lovely birthday dinner. She'd gone to her room, but too keyed up to go to bed, she'd decided to go for a walk.

She pulled her jacket on over her new dress, a birthday gift from Tobias, and began to wander through the orchard that spread out behind the house. The night was cold and snow lay on the ground, but she hadn't minded as she let her thoughts drift over the evening.

Half an hour later, feeling a little chilled, she made her way back to the house. As she slipped through the gate at the entrance to the orchard, she heard Drew drive up.

She smiled a greeting as she walked toward his car. She hadn't seen him leave earlier and when he stepped from the car she was surprised to see he was wearing a black tuxedo with a white ruffled shirt and a black bow tie. She remembered thinking, as he returned her smile, that he looked like a famous movie star—tall, dark and incredibly handsome.

"How was your birthday dinner, shrimp?" he asked.

"Wonderful," she told him. "But we missed you."

"Where did you go? Dimitri's?" Drew asked as they walked toward the kitchen door.

"No, we went to that new restaurant, The Salamander," she told him. "You should have been there, Drew, they have a dance floor...and live music. It was lovely," she added with a wistful sigh.

"Did you dance?" Drew asked, a teasing smile tugging at the corners of his mouth.

Vienna shook her head. "I asked Tobias, but he said he was too old."

"I'm not too old," Drew announced. "And I think every girl who reaches the ripe old age of sixteen should have at least one dance on her birthday. Shall we give it a whirl?"

"You mean right now?" she asked, laughter welling up inside her.

"Of course," came Drew's reply, and before she could take a breath, he pulled her into his arms and began to waltz around the yard.

At first, Vienna felt silly and awkward, and the snow made things a little slippery. But in a matter of moments she was keeping step with Drew as he spun her around and around.

When at last they came to a halt she was dizzy and they were both out of breath. She stumbled against him, and his arms tightened around her, making her feel warm and secure. Still trying to catch her breath, she lifted her head to look at Drew. When their eyes met, she felt as if she'd been struck by a bolt of lightning. An electrical charge seemed to pass right through her. The sensation was like nothing she'd ever experienced before, and as those endless seconds ticked by, she was aware of only the frantic beating of her heart against her rib cage.

Seconds later, Drew was holding her away from him, his eyes as black as the sky behind him. Her own heart, body and soul were in total confusion, and she'd had to bite down on her lower lip to stop it from trembling.

"That's enough dancing for one night," Drew said lightly, but the smile that followed didn't quite reach his eyes. "You'd better go inside and get to bed, young lady, before you freeze to death. I'll be right there—I forgot my coat." He turned and made his way back to his car.

Vienna wasn't sure how she'd made it into the house or even up to her room. She'd spent a sleepless night, confused about what had happened outside, but knowing that for her, nothing would be quite the same again.

But that was ten years ago, Vienna reminded herself, and she was no longer the starry-eyed teenager who'd had a secret crush on Drew. With this thought planted firmly in her mind, she climbed out of the bathtub and wrapped the soft towel around her.

She was overwrought—that was all. During the past week she'd been through so much, emotionally. Drew's arrival and presence had simply triggered old, forgotten memories and emotions, bringing them to the fore. She would simply have to lock them away again—only much more securely this time.

Back in her room, Vienna slipped into her undergarments. After a moment's hesitation, she put on the silky red dress Bruce had suggested she wear for their date tonight. Its style was simple yet elegant, with a scoop neckline, long, fitted sleeves, a belted waist and a full skirt that ended just below her knees.

Vienna carefully applied a minimum of makeup, ran a brush through her black curls, and reached for the bottle of her favorite perfume.

As she made her way downstairs, she felt a little more in control, quietly assuring herself that a romantic evening with Bruce was exactly what she needed to boost her spirits and make her forget her silly notions about Drew.

She pinned a smile on her face as she pushed open the kitchen door, and immediately she was met with a tantalizing aroma.

Daisy and Buffy, stretched out under the table, scrambled to their feet and, tails wagging, came forward to greet her. Vienna patted both dogs, then glanced at Drew, who stood with his back to her, staring thoughtfully out the kitchen window.

He turned and immediately his glance traveled the length of her, over the full curve of her breasts down to the gentle swell of her hips and back again to her face. She held her breath, aware of the wild, erratic beating of her heart. Her skin tingled in response to the appreciation she could see in his eyes, and the air seemed to crackle with tension.

When Daisy gently nudged Vienna's hand with her wet nose, she glanced down at the dog, infinitely glad of the distraction.

"You want to go out, don't you, girl?" Vienna's voice trembled a little. At her words, Daisy ambled toward the back door and Vienna followed. "Come on, Buffy, you too," she said, and the little dog followed Daisy into the darkness.

A flurry of cold air danced across her skin and Vienna quickly closed the door and turned around. "I'm glad to see you've made yourself at home," she said, striving to keep her tone casual. "But then, you always did like to cook." She crossed to the stove next to the sink. "What is it?" she asked, reaching for the lid of one of the pots.

Drew joined her at the stove. He removed the lid from her fingers and replaced it. "It's only a meat stew," he replied. "I used almost everything you had in the fridge. I hope you don't mind."

"Of course not," she chided softly, turning to face him. "I'll shop tomorrow. It smells wonderful." She tried to ignore the flutter of nerves that had erupted in her stomach as a direct result of his nearness.

"So do you," he quickly countered, his lips curling into a smile. "I'm amazed at all the changes that have taken place in the last eight years." His eyes captured hers in a look that sent her pulse racing. "I almost didn't recognize you just now. All grown-up at last. Congratulations," he said, and before she could speak or react, he leaned toward her, brushing her lips with his.

The kiss, light and featherlike, ended almost as soon as it began. Yet the moment his mouth touched hers, Vienna's body quivered in instant response. She gave a whimper as he pulled away, and the sound brought Drew's dark eyes to hers once more.

For a long, timeless second their gazes locked, then with a muttered curse, he brought his mouth unerringly down on hers.

Shock ricocheted through her at the bruising pressure of his lips, but the pain was only fleeting, quickly swept away by the powerful, overwhelming sensations that followed in its wake. She'd never known that a kiss could offer so much, and promise even more. The heat, the urgency, seemed to consume her and as her hands traced a path across his back, she could feel the latent strength and primitive power of him beneath her fingers.

There was a sense of urgency, even desperation, in his kiss, and Vienna responded with all the generosity her heart could offer. And for the first time in her life, she realized just how much she had longed to be in Drew's arms. She clung to him, savoring the heady taste and tantalizing sensations his kiss evoked, never wanting the moment to end. But it was over all too soon when the dogs began to bark outside, signaling someone's arrival.

Drew instantly broke the kiss, but he didn't move away. Instead he gazed intently at her flushed face. For Vienna, it was small consolation to note that his breathing was as ragged as her own, but the anger she could see in the depths of his eyes and the taut line of his jaw sent a pain slicing through her.

"Sounds like your date has arrived," Drew said tightly, drawing a little farther away with each word he spoke. "I'm not sure whether to apologize to you or to him," he added, as a knock sounded at the door. He glanced at the door, then back at her. "On second thought, I think I'll go and see what Chris is up to. I never was much good at apologizing. Have a nice evening," he added, before turning and heading for the stairs.

Vienna stood in frozen silence, watching Drew leave. Her emotions were in total chaos, whereas in contrast, Drew seemed very much in control. Had she been the only one affected by the kiss?

The question was quickly pushed aside as another knock sounded, this time louder. Vienna forced herself to go to the door, and tried to gather her scattered wits.

"Hi!" Bruce greeted her with a grin. "You look stunning, darling." He leaned toward her, but Vienna quickly turned her head so that the kiss landed on her cheek.

"Thank you," she said, and even managed a smile as she eased away from him. "I'll just get my coat," she added and hurried out into the hallway.

Why had she avoided his kiss just now? Bruce had kissed her before, and she'd always found the experience warm and pleasant. But not earth-shattering, a tiny voice inside her head pointed out.

Angry now, Vienna put on her coat and thrust all thoughts of Drew aside as she returned to the kitchen, telling herself that she would not allow one small insignificant kiss to spoil an entire evening. As Bruce held the car door for her and she settled into the plush seat, a dull but persistent ache took up residence inside her head.

As the evening progressed, the strain of pretending she was enjoying herself became more and more difficult. She hardly touched the food set before her, and though she tried to listen to Bruce and make suitable comments, the fact that he'd brought her to The Salamander seemed somehow to undermine her earlier resolve.

Bruce was attentive and charming, but throughout dinner Vienna found her thoughts continually straying to Drew.

"You seem a little preoccupied tonight," Bruce said, and guiltily she brought her attention back to the man opposite.

"I'm sorry." She felt her face grow warm under his gaze.

"You're not still worried about Tobias, are you? He's doing fine...talking nonstop about that grandson of his."

Vienna shook her head, but before she could speak, the waiter appeared to clear their plates. Glad of the interruption, she reached for the glass of wine she'd barely touched.

After the waiter departed, Vienna determinedly changed the subject. "I seem to remember you saying something about tonight being a special evening," she said.

"That's right," Bruce answered, a triumphant smile tugging at his mouth.

"You got that promotion! Oh, Bruce, I forgot all about it. I'm so sorry." She felt decidedly annoyed with herself. He'd applied for a post on the hospital administration board over a month ago, but she'd completely forgotten to ask whether or not he'd been successful.

"That's all right. They took their time about making the decision," he explained. "I'd just about given up hope."

"Congratulations," she said. Smiling now, she raised her wineglass and touched his, before taking a sip.

"Thank you. But I was hoping we could make this a double celebration," he went on.

"Oh," Vienna said softly, a sinking feeling suddenly descending on her. Bruce put his hand in his jacket pocket and brought out a small velvet box.

"I was going to wait until your birthday to give you this, but I'll be at that medical seminar in Vancouver then. When they told me today I had the job in administration...well, I thought that tonight would be as good a time as any—" His hand came out to capture one of hers, and Vienna had to swallow deeply before she could raise her eyes to meet his.

"Bruce...I..."

"Will you marry me?" He opened the box and the diamond inside sparkled invitingly at her.

Vienna stared in stunned silence. If he'd given her the ring two weeks ago, perhaps even two days ago, she could almost convince herself she would have accepted it—almost.

During the past six months since she'd started going out with Bruce, she'd often asked herself if the warmth and friendship she felt for him was really love.

Throughout school and at veterinary college, she'd been too busy with her studies to take time out for love or romance. As a result, at twenty-six she was totally inexperienced, and when Bruce began pressuring her into a more intimate relationship, she'd tried to tell herself that it was simply her lack of experience that prevented her from giving in to his demands.

She liked Bruce—he was fun to be with, they got along well, and she found his kisses pleasant and satisfying, but... But his kisses had never turned her world upside down, had never shaken her to the core, awakening emotions she was afraid to face or analyze. And suddenly she realized that some indefinable element was missing from her feelings for Bruce.

Her mouth felt dry as parchment, and a sadness curled around her heart as she searched for the right words to tell him she couldn't accept.

"It would seem I'm a little premature," he said, a trace of frustration in his tone.

She kept her gaze level with his. "Bruce...it's just that—"

"I know. You've been upset about Tobias," he cut in. "But I thought this was the next step in our relationship, that this was what you wanted...."

Vienna couldn't for the life of her think of anything to say. He was right; she had been thinking about making a commitment, until Drew arrived— until Drew kissed her....

Bruce closed the ring box with a snap and put it back in his pocket. Leaning across the table, he took her hands in his and when he spoke, his tone was soft and coaxing. "Will you think about it? I'm leaving tomorrow night for Vancouver, and I won't be back until the beginning of next week."

"Bruce . . ." she began.

"Please, just think about it," he repeated. "That's not too much to ask, is it?"

Vienna shook her head. At the very least, he was her friend. Even though she knew her answer would be the same when he returned, she couldn't bring herself to say the words she knew would hurt him.

"It's been a rather hectic day. If you don't mind, I'd like to go home."

"Of course."

The journey there was completed in silence and as Bruce brought the car to a halt, she stole a glance at him. He turned to her and before she could stop him, he leaned over and covered her mouth with his.

"Good night, Vienna. Sweet dreams," he said softly, when he drew away.

"Good night," Vienna managed, and quickly made her escape.

As she reached the door, she heard the car drive away but she didn't turn around. His kiss just now had been as brief as the one she'd shared earlier with Drew, but that was the only comparison she could make. With Bruce there had been none of the heat and excitement Drew's kiss had aroused so easily and so swiftly. She'd felt nothing—no quickening of her heart, no new and exciting sensations clamoring to life within her—nothing.

With a tired sigh, Vienna quietly let herself into the house.

"Well, well. Just the person I wanted to see." Drew's voice startled Vienna out of her reverie. She glanced up to see him seated at the kitchen table with a file folder open in front of him.

"What is it? What happened?" she asked anxiously.

"I was hoping you'd tell me," came his reply.

Chapter Seven

"Is it Tobias? Is he all right?"

"He's fine," Drew calmly assured her. "He was a little tired tonight. We didn't stay long."

Relief swept through Vienna to be replaced almost instantly with annoyance. "Then would you kindly explain what this is all about?" she asked, coming farther into the room.

"I'd be happy to. But first I have some questions that need answering."

"Questions?" she repeated. "What about?"

Suddenly, the sound of whining and scratching reached Vienna and immediately she crossed to let the dogs out of the room where they spent the night. Daisy and Buffy greeted her excitedly, their tails wagging frantically as she bent to pat them.

"I made a pot of coffee earlier," Drew said abruptly. "Would you like a cup?"

"Yes, all right," she said—a trifle reluctantly, since the idea of spending time alone with Drew was already beginning to create a tension within her.

Drew rose and went to the stove. "And how was your evening with the good doctor?" he asked, a hint of mockery in his tone.

"Great, thank you," she said, forcing a note of enthusiasm into her voice. But as her thoughts turned to Bruce, feelings of guilt and sadness returned anew, and she found herself wishing life wasn't quite so complicated. She murmured soft commands to the dogs to lie down, and with a sigh slipped off her coat and dropped it over one of the kitchen chairs.

"With sugar, right?" Drew asked.

"Yes," she replied, surprised and faintly pleased that he remembered. Pulling a chair out from the table, she sat down.

Drew set the cup in front of her and returned to his seat.

"Thank you," she said, and taking a sip, she glanced across at Drew. "You said you had some questions."

He studied her for a long moment, and under the sharp scrutiny of his gaze, Vienna felt her pulse accelerate and a warmth spread through her.

"Did you know that Tobias has missed half-a-dozen loan payments to the bank, and now they're threatening to foreclose on the house and orchards unless the arrears are paid by the end of the month?"

Vienna stared in utter astonishment at Drew. "But that's impossible!" she burst out. Surely Tobias would have said something to her. It couldn't be true, could it? But the hard expression in Drew's eyes told her he wasn't lying. "How? I mean, it doesn't make sense. Tobias never said a word to me...." Her voice grew faint.

"It's right here in black-and-white," he said, picking up a letter from atop the pile of papers on the table. He offered it to her.

Vienna reached across and took it from him. She quickly scanned the contents, which merely confirmed what he'd already told her.

"This letter is dated a few days before Tobias had his heart attack," she said, glancing again at Drew.

"That's right," he acknowledged in a tight voice.

"Dear heaven...this is probably what brought on the attack in the first place. It *has* to be."

"But you knew nothing about this?" The hint of accusation in Drew's tone immediately brought her attention back to him.

She met his gaze head-on. "Don't you think if I'd known, I would have tried to do something?" she said defensively. "You, of all people, Drew, know how stubborn Tobias can be. I'm only his goddaughter. He never talked to me about his financial situation. Besides, it's really none of my business."

Drew pushed his chair back and stood up. He dragged his hand through his hair and gave a tired sigh. Watching him, Vienna noticed the lines of concern on his face, and her anger evaporated. That Drew cared about his father was obvious. She felt hope stir inside her that a reconciliation might indeed be possible—if only they weren't both so stubborn.

"How did you find out about this?" she asked suddenly, as she glanced down at the papers on the table. "Where did you get that file? What were you doing looking through your father's private papers?"

Drew ran his hand across the back of his neck, as if to ease a knot of tension. "When Chris and I were at the hospital earlier, I casually asked my father how business was."

"What did he say?"

"He practically snapped my head off, told me to mind my own business. He was obviously upset, and so I let the matter drop. Then, when Chris started telling him all about Rags, he seemed relieved at the change of subject." Drew came to a halt and leaned against the counter. "For the rest of the visit, he hardly spoke a word to me. I couldn't shake the feeling that something was wrong. A little later he said he was tired. We took the hint and left. But all the way home, I couldn't stop thinking about his reaction to what I thought was an innocent question. After Chris went to bed, I decided to take a look upstairs in Tobias's office."

"And you found this," Vienna said, tapping the letter.

"Yes. That file was lying on his desk. According to these records, two years ago he lost his entire peach crop, as well as most of his pears, to an early frost. For a small operation like this, one bad season is all it takes to put you in the red. Using the house and orchards as collateral, he secured a loan from the bank. But I gather that it must have been an uphill battle since then to make the loan payments."

Vienna frowned. "That must have happened the summer I was offered a job in a veterinary practice near the college," she reflected aloud. "Tobias was great about it—he said he understood. I didn't come home for a holiday until Thanksgiving, but he didn't say anything. If I hadn't taken that job, I'd have been here...."

"And just how the hell do you think I feel?" Drew's angry tone sliced through her, bringing her head up. "Have you any idea how many times during the past eight years I've wanted to come home?" There was a bitter edge to his voice, and the pain she could see etched on his face told a story of its own.

He was standing gripping the back of the chair he'd vacated only a few minutes earlier, but he seemed not to see her as he continued. "Tobias was right—" Drew spoke the words with resignation "—I should never have gone off with Natalie . . . should never have married her. She seemed to think I had an endless supply of cash, but by the time we reached Los Angeles we were nearly broke. She kept telling me to use my credit cards, but I refused because I knew that Tobias would have to pay the bills. And I was damned if—" He broke off abruptly. "She soon became bored and restless. I managed to get a job, but that didn't help for long. Six months later, she ran off with a rich guy and left me a note telling me not to bother looking for her.

"By that time I'd had about enough myself. I'd been working at a job I detested, and coming home to a dingy little apartment and a wife who spent her day watching TV and reading glossy magazines we couldn't afford to buy.'' He drew a ragged breath. ''After she left, I took every last penny I had and bought a plane ticket home.'' He stopped and stared into space, his knuckles white with strain. ''Then I remembered the words my father shouted at me right here in this kitchen the day Natalie and I left. 'Don't come crawling back here,' he'd said.'' Drew released his hold on the chair and began to turn away.

Vienna jumped to her feet and moved toward him, wanting to ease at least some of the pain he was reliving. ''Tobias was angry, he was hurt—''

''So was I,'' Drew cut in, his eyes meeting hers. ''I knew then and there, I couldn't come back. I had to prove to myself that I could make it on my own. Leaving home had been easy,'' he went on, weariness in his voice now. ''Staying away was the most difficult thing I've ever had to do.''

Emotion formed a knot in Vienna's throat at the agony and guilt she could see in the depths of his dark eyes. She couldn't speak, so she reached out to touch his arm.

''Don't,'' she pleaded softly. ''Drew, don't do this to yourself.''

Without a second thought, her arms went around him and she held him to her. It was a gesture that was meant solely to comfort, to ease at least some of the pain and tension she could feel inside him.

Several seconds ticked by before she felt him gradually begin to relax and his arms slowly encircled her. But it was during these seconds that Vienna suddenly found herself struggling to ignore the feel of his body pressed firmly against hers. The rich, masculine scent of him was deliciously intoxicating, and the rough texture of his chin where it rested against her forehead was eliciting strange and exciting responses somewhere deep inside her.

She had the strongest urge to press her body closer to his, to hold on tighter, to kiss the strong column of his neck that was so enticingly near. She felt sure he must hear the way her heart was pounding against her ribs. Being held in Drew's arms was suddenly a tantalizing torture, playing havoc with her senses and awakening needs she'd never known before.

Then Drew pulled away, holding her at arm's length. As their gazes locked she realized that he, too, was remembering the kiss they'd shared earlier. The tension between them was almost tangible and her heart stopped in midbeat before racing on like an overworked metronome.

Drew dropped his hands to his sides and took a step back. There was to be no repeat of the kiss. Now that she was no longer in his arms, Vienna felt strangely bereft, totally unprepared for the disappointment that tugged at her heart.

"This is getting us nowhere." Drew's deep voice was cool and controlled. "Feeling guilty is a waste of time and energy, and certainly won't do my father a damn bit of good."

Pride and stubbornness won't help, either, Vienna wanted to say; but she remained silent, fighting her own battle with emotions gone disastrously awry.

"I'll talk to Tobias tomorrow," Drew continued. "The letter from the bank says he has until the end of the month to make good those loan payments and—"

"But you can't talk to him about it," Vienna cut in, fear and anxiety for Tobias rising to the surface now. "You mustn't! Don't you see?" she said. "Worrying about this business with the bank is obviously what put Tobias in the hospital in the first place. If you confront him now, he's likely to suffer another attack."

"Hey! Take it easy, take it easy," said Drew, and Vienna caught the glimmer of amusement in the mysterious depths of his eyes. "I see you're still as fiercely protective of him as ever. But this time I agree, you have a point. We'll just have to find another way to deal with this."

Vienna breathed a sigh of relief, and smiled at the way Drew had so casually used the word *we*. It was utterly foolish to read more into it, but she felt warmed by the fact that he'd listened to her objection and acceded to her reasoning.

"Make an appointment with the bank manager," she suggested. "Surely he'll be able to tell you what you need to know."

"I'll do that tomorrow," Drew said, a fleeting smile lifting the corners of his mouth. "Actually, I was sitting here puzzling over this before you arrived, and I have an idea that might be worth exploring," he added, his expression thoughtful now.

"What is it? Tell me," she asked eagerly.

But Drew shook his head. "All in good time. At the moment it's only an idea. I don't want to raise any false hopes."

Vienna opened her mouth to ask more, but Drew brought a finger to her lips, effectively silencing her.

His finger lingered a moment too long and the tingling awareness she'd experienced only moments ago returned a hundredfold.

She watched as Drew withdrew his hand and his expression darkened. When he spoke, his tone was abrupt.

"It's late, I'll say goodnight." With this, he turned and made his way from the room, leaving her alone with emotions that were still churning.

She busied herself clearing away the coffee mugs and then she let the dogs out for their final run, all the while keeping her thoughts away from Drew and focused on Tobias.

Why hadn't Tobias talked to her? Why hadn't he told her he was in trouble? As these questions circled in her head, she had to fight the feelings of guilt that threatened to return. But any doubts she might still have had about the wisdom of calling California and letting Drew know about Tobias were obliterated now. And she had every confidence that Tobias's future would be safe in Drew's capable hands. She trusted Drew, had always trusted him. And even though she hadn't seen him for eight years, she felt confident that he was still the kind of man who would not easily break a trust.

If Drew managed to resolve Tobias's problems, she could only pray that it might lead to a reconciliation between him and his father.

"Vienna, wake up! It's snowing." The excited voice outside her bedroom door belonged to Chris. Vienna pushed back the covers and reached for her robe. She crossed to the window, and as she tied the sash of her dressing gown she smiled. The world outside looked as if it had been lightly dusted with powdered sugar.

She opened her door, but there was no sign of Chris. All she could hear was the sound of footsteps thundering down the stairs. She was about to turn back into her room when the bathroom door opposite her opened.

Drew stopped in the doorway and began to vigorously towel-dry his hair, unaware of her presence. His chest was bare and he wore a pair of pale blue denims that hung loosely on his hips, accentuating the narrowness of his waist. Fine black hairs curled across his chest, tapering downward to disappear beneath the waistband of his jeans.

Vienna felt as if she'd been scorched by a hot flame, as the impact of seeing Drew's naked torso sent a dizzying heat spiraling through her. Before he caught sight of her, she quickly closed the door then leaned against it for support.

Dear heaven! What was happening to her? she wondered dazedly as she waited for the tide of heat and longing racing through her to subside. Never before could she recall reacting so strongly to the sight of a man's half-naked body.

Not until she heard Drew's heavy footsteps on the stairs did she venture from her room. Even then, she lingered in the bathroom longer than usual, decidedly reluctant to face him. When she could put it off no longer, she made her way to the kitchen.

"But I don't want to go to school. I want to go with Vienna and help her look after Rags," Chris was saying when she entered, and Vienna heard the note of defiance in his voice.

"Sorry, sport, but I just talked to the principal and it's all settled," Drew answered calmly. "If we're going to be staying here for another week—and that's the way things are shaping up at the moment—then I feel you've missed enough school already."

"But I won't know anybody," Chris argued, glaring at his father with an expression that reminded Vienna so much of Drew.

"You'll know Tim," she said as she crossed to the sink. "I'll bet you might even be in his class. You liked him, didn't you?"

"Yeah...I guess," Chris conceded.

"School will be closing for the Christmas holidays in a couple of weeks," she went on, as she popped two pieces of bread into the toaster. "And there are usually lots of fun things going on at this time of year, like making decorations, and singing carols...."

"Well...I suppose it won't be too bad if Tim's going to be there," Chris muttered as he put the last spoonful of cereal into his mouth.

He chewed thoughtfully for a few moments. Over his head, Vienna caught sight of Drew's grateful smile. Her heart skipped a beat, and it was all she could do to nod in acknowledgement before turning her attention back to the toaster.

"Your father can drop us at the clinic," suggested Vienna a few minutes later. "That way you can look in on Rags first, then you and Tim can walk to school together."

"Okay," agreed Chris, this time with a little more enthusiasm.

"I'll come and pick you both up at the clinic after school," Drew said. "Then we can pop in at the hospital and see Tobias before we head home."

"Fine," said Vienna as she poured herself a cup of coffee. It was strange how making these simple arrangements should give her the impression that they were almost a real family. A faint longing tugged at her heart at this idea, and she quickly had to remind herself that the situation was only a temporary one.

"When does the bank open? Ten?" Drew asked, breaking into her thoughts.

"Yes," she replied. Coffee cup in one hand and a plate of toast in the other, she crossed to the table and sat down.

"Can I go outside and play with the dogs until it's time to go?" Chris asked as he pushed his plate aside.

"Yes, just make sure you dress warmly," Drew told him, but Chris was already out of his chair and racing toward the hallway.

Twenty minutes later, with the dogs fed and settled in their room for the day, Vienna handed Drew the keys to the station wagon, and with Chris in the back seat, they set off.

For the remainder of the week, their days fell into something of a pattern. Each morning, Drew would drop them off at the clinic and return in the late afternoon to take them to the hospital to visit Tobias.

When he'd picked them up that first day, Vienna had asked how his interview with the bank manager had gone. Drew had told her the meeting had gone reasonably well, but when she'd pressed him for more details he'd asked her to be patient. He'd said he'd called his office in San Francisco and had put someone to work on the idea he'd mentioned.

Tobias continued to show improvement, but there was still a lingering anxiety in the older man's eyes. Vienna knew that it had to do with his worry over the bank's threat to foreclose. She wished she could tell Tobias that Drew had taken charge of things, but she was afraid that if she brought up the topic, he might suffer a relapse.

That Tobias enjoyed their visits, and in particular Chris's company, was obvious. The friendship developing between grandfather and grandson was a joy to see.

Vienna sensed that Drew found the visits with his father something of a strain. Each time they returned to the house, he would immediately shut himself in Tobias's office, where he spent a good deal of time talking on the telephone. The sad consequence of this was that he spent very little time with Chris.

Vienna remembered all too clearly her own childhood, and the loneliness she'd experienced. Christmas was fast approaching, and as yet Drew hadn't followed through on his suggestion to take Chris to the mall to see Santa. As each day passed, she could see anticipation and excitement growing in Chris; and each time she caught him looking at his father, she saw a longing in his eyes that spoke volumes.

While Drew didn't exactly ignore the boy, he didn't seek him out or pay special attention to him, and Vienna wondered if Drew realized just how much his actions affected Chris. Though she knew that Drew was simply engrossed in the problems facing Tobias, her sympathies lay with Chris. He was becoming very attached to Tobias, to Rags, and even to her. She couldn't help thinking that when the time came for Drew and Chris to return to California, Chris would resent his father for taking him away from here.

In effect, Drew seemed to have forgotten his resolve to bridge the gap between him and his son. Perhaps it was time for her to remind him.

It was Friday afternoon and Vienna was waiting for Drew to arrive. During the past week, business at the clinic had picked up and there were several animals in the cages, awaiting their owners.

Chris and Tim were outside with Rags, playing in the snow-covered lot at the rear of the building. The boys had promised not to let the young dog get too rambunctious, but Rags was improving and growing more restless and in need of exercise each day.

Rags had made a good recovery, thanks in part to Chris's love and attention. The dog's coat was slowly beginning to grow over the scar, but the wound would never be completely invisible.

That Chris loved Rags was unmistakable, and while she knew she shouldn't encourage this particular relationship, Vienna couldn't find it in her heart to begin looking for a new home for the dog—at least not yet.

The outer door opened and Chris, Tim and Rags came in.

"Isn't he here yet?" Chris asked, with the note of annoyance in his voice that was sometimes evident when he spoke to or about his father.

"Not yet," Vienna answered, glancing up at the clock on the wall.

"I'd better go," Tim said. "It's almost time for supper."

"See you later, Tim," Chris called after his friend.

Rags lay down on the floor, panting. He looked a picture of health and Vienna couldn't help smiling, remembering clearly how he'd looked the morning Sam Williamson had brought him in. There was nothing more rewarding than seeing an animal regain its health and strength.

Chris sank down beside Rags and the dog's tail immediately began to thump against the floor. He gazed adoringly at Chris and his tongue came out to lick the boy's hand. "I wish my dad would let me keep Rags," Chris said wistfully, voicing the thought that slipped all too often into her own head whenever she saw Chris and Rags together.

"Couldn't we take him home with us tonight?" Chris asked. "He doesn't like that cage anymore. I could look after him. He wouldn't fight with Daisy or Buffy. He likes other dogs."

"I just don't think your father would approve," said Vienna reluctantly. But she had to agree with Chris—it was no longer fair to the dog to keep him confined at the clinic each night.

"What wouldn't I approve of?" The sound of Drew's deep voice startled her and immediately she turned around to find him standing in the open doorway, with a bouquet of flowers in his hand.

Chapter Eight

Vienna's heart skipped a beat at the sight of Drew—his face partially hidden by the flowers and the trace of a smile curling at his mouth.

"What wouldn't I approve of?" he asked again, as the door closed behind him.

"Rags is much better now," Chris said as he jumped up from the floor and faced his father. "And it isn't fair to keep him here in a cage anymore. I asked Vienna if he could come home with us tonight. But she told me..."

"I wouldn't approve," Drew finished for him.

"I promise I'll keep him out of your way. He'll be good." Chris pleaded his case.

Drew's expression changed, and if there had been a smile a moment ago, it was gone now. "Chris, you're getting much too attached to Rags, and when the time comes for us to go back to California, not only will it be hard on you, but on the dog, as well.''

"I don't want to leave. I like it here with Vienna and Gramps,'' Chris said, anger and frustration evident in his voice.

"Chris . . .'' Vienna cautioned, even as she saw the look of pain that flashed across Drew's features.

"I don't want to argue tonight,'' Drew said. "Not when we have a birthday to celebrate.''

"A birthday? Whose birthday?'' Chris asked, unable to ignore his father's remark.

"Vienna's,'' Drew replied. "These are for you, birthday girl.'' He held out the flowers to her.

The sudden tightness in Vienna's throat made it impossible for her to speak. Furiously she blinked away the tears stinging her eyes and managed to smile as she took the bouquet from Drew.

"Happy Birthday, Vienna,'' Chris chimed as he came to stand beside her. "I'm sorry I don't have a present for you,'' he added, "but I didn't know.''

"That's all right, Chris.'' Vienna smiled down at him. Her heart was tripping over itself in confusion as she tried to deal with the fact that Drew had remembered her birthday. As she inhaled the mildly spicy fragrance of the pink and white carnations, she couldn't describe the array of emotions washing over her.

"Thank you, Drew,'' she murmured, managing at last to meet his gaze. He was smiling now, and the warmth she could see in his eyes only served to send a frisson of awareness through her.

"The celebration has only just begun," Drew said. "Chris, what do you say we take Vienna out for a birthday dinner?"

"Yeah!" Chris replied eagerly. "That could be her present, right?"

"Good thinking." Drew grinned at his son. "I thought you might agree with me, so I booked a table at The Salamander. But we'd better get cracking." He glanced at his watch. "We just have enough time to go home and get changed."

"You mean we have to get all dressed up?" Chris asked, his enthusiasm waning a little.

"Of course!" Drew flashed a smile at Vienna.

"But what about Gramps?" Chris asked suddenly.

"Gramps knows all about it. I just came from the hospital. That's why I'm a little late."

"How is he feeling today?" Vienna asked.

"The same as ever," Drew replied, and noticing the subdued note in his voice, Vienna gave an inward sigh. Since his arrival, Drew had visited his father every day, but it was obvious from his remark that the barriers were still in place and that nothing had really changed. He was making as little progress with his father as he was with Chris.

"Drew, listen, it really isn't necessary to take me out—"

"Nonsense! When I told Tobias about the plans I'd made, he approved wholeheartedly. Besides, birthday dinners are something of a tradition in this family, remember?"

At these words, Vienna found herself blinking back tears once more. Since her father's death, Tobias had welcomed her into his home with open arms, and she'd soon learned that birthdays, hers included, were indeed a special occasion in the Sheridan household.

"But what about Rags?" Chris ventured. "Can we take him home with us?"

Vienna turned to him. "Not tonight, Chris," she said, and softened her words with a smile. "It wouldn't be fair to leave him with the other dogs, now that we're going out."

Chris sighed. "I guess you're right," he said as he bent to scratch Rags's ears. "Come on, boy... bedtime." Obediently Rags followed Chris from the room.

When the boy returned a few moments later, his expression was sad. As Vienna locked the doors behind them, she glanced at Drew, wondering if he heard the heart-wrenching sound of Rags whining and crying.

Bright Christmas lights were strung across the roof of The Salamander and they twinkled a welcome as Drew pulled the wagon into an empty parking space on the street.

Inside the restaurant's front door stood a gigantic Christmas tree, beautifully trimmed with delicate ornaments and colored balls that shimmered under the lights.

"Vienna! Back again, are you?" Janice Clarkson, a hostess at the restaurant, greeted her. "I thought Bruce was in Vancouver— Oh! I'm sorry," the woman glanced at Drew and then at Vienna.

"That's all right. Janice, I'd like you to meet Drew, Tobias's son," she explained, glad that the lighting was dim enough to help hide the blush creeping over her face.

"Welcome to The Salamander," said Janice with a smile. "I hope Tobias is feeling better and will be out of the hospital soon."

"Thank you," said Drew, but there was no answering smile, and Vienna found herself wondering if she was simply imagining the tension in the air.

"Please follow me. Your table is ready," Janice went on, in a businesslike tone.

As she followed Janice to their table, Vienna found herself thinking back to the evening when she'd had dinner here with Bruce.

She was ashamed to admit that since that night she'd hardly thought about Bruce or his proposal, and she knew that the reason for this had everything to do with Drew. His presence and the depth of emotion he could so easily arouse in her had forced her to closely examine her feelings for Bruce. Now she knew, beyond the shadow of a doubt, that what she felt for Bruce was simply a deep friendship and nothing more.

It had surprised her how relieved she'd felt at this discovery. But what she found distressing was that she'd been on the brink of accepting Bruce's proposal. Though she knew her refusal would hurt him, there was some consolation in the knowledge that he deserved more than she could give him. He deserved a woman who loved him.

"Would you care for a drink from the bar before dinner?" the waitress asked, cutting through her thoughts. Vienna shook her head and turned her attention to the menu in her hands.

"A cola, please," Chris said.

Vienna smiled and glanced at Chris, who was now gazing around at the other tables, his eyes wide with curiosity and unabashed interest. Dressed in black pants and a bright red sweater, and with his hair brushed back from his face, he looked like a smaller version of his father.

Turning her attention to Drew now, she studied him surreptitiously. Like Chris's, his thick black hair was brushed away from his face, showing it to full advantage, but there was a maturity and masculinity in his handsome features that were, as yet, lacking in the boy's.

Dark eyebrows hooded blue-black eyes that with one look could make her skin tingle and her heart race. His nose was straight and his skin was lightly tanned. His jaw looked invitingly smooth, with only the hint of a shadow. Vienna let her gaze linger for a moment on the strong line of his jaw before her eyes came, at last, to his mouth.

She hadn't realized she'd been holding her breath until she felt her heart kick against her ribcage in reaction to her unhurried appraisal. And suddenly she found herself remembering all too clearly the way his lips had felt pressed firmly against hers. Her face grew warm at the memory and she quickly closed her eyes, annoyed at herself now as she struggled to regain some semblance of control.

"Have you decided what you want?" Drew asked, and her eyes flew open at his words. He was talking to

Chris, and as Vienna tried to slow her heartbeat, she lowered her head to hide her confusion.

"Can I have a steak? I've never had one in a restaurant before."

"Then steak it shall be," Drew said easily, and Vienna looked up in time to catch father and son exchange fleeting smiles.

A pain tugged at her heartstrings, and not for the first time she wondered if Drew realized just how much Chris wanted and needed his acceptance and approval. She knew that the defiance Chris often showed was simply a means of defense. She'd acted that way on occasion when she'd been his age, in a vain attempt to gain her parents' attention. She'd been starved for affection and crying out for love, and she knew instinctively that Chris was experiencing the same needs.

"What about you, Vienna?" Drew focused his dark eyes on hers, sending her pulse tripping into high gear.

"Steak sounds great," she said, closing the menu, relieved to note that Drew seemed relaxed now.

"In that case, I'll order a bottle of Cabernet...Californian, of course," he added with a smile.

"That would be lovely," Vienna said, thinking that she didn't need wine—Drew's smile was intoxicating enough.

While Drew ordered for all of them, she turned to Chris. "What did you do in school today?"

"We did some printing in our writing books, and then math," said Chris, with a frown. "But in the afternoon we made some decorations for the tree, then

Mrs. Lucas read us a story,'' he added in a brighter tone.

"A Christmas story, I bet," Vienna remarked. "Those are my favorite."

"Me, too," Chris agreed. "Oh, look, the band's going to play," he said excitedly, pointing to the small stage across the room. Vienna and Drew turned to follow his gaze.

"They play here every Friday and Saturday night," Vienna explained. "There's a small dance floor on the other side of the stage."

"You mean people come here to dance?" Chris asked, his tone disbelieving.

"That's right," she replied, trying not to smile.

The band consisted of two guitarists, a piano player and a drummer, and after a few minutes the soft strains of a well-known Christmas song drifted across the room.

Vienna sighed. "I can't believe Christmas is nearly here. Do you think Tobias will be released from the hospital in time for Christmas?"

"I don't see why not," Drew replied. "He's making steady progress, and getting a little restless, too. I heard him asking one of the nurses when he could get out of bed."

"Are we spending Christmas here with Vienna and Gramps?" Chris asked suddenly, his eyes intent on Drew.

Drew took a deep breath before answering. "I'm not sure—"

"I want to stay. I like it here." There was a challenge in Chris's voice.

"I'm glad you like it here, Chris," said Drew, his tone sincere. "But unfortunately, things don't always work out the way you want them to." Before he could say more, the waitress returned with their meals.

Vienna focused her attention on the food on her plate. She was surprised at how much both Drew and Chris had come to mean to her in the short time they'd been here. But she'd do well to keep reminding herself that their stay was not permanent. This thought brought a stab of pain to her heart.

She felt sure that one of the reasons Chris wanted to stay in Peachville had to do with Tobias and the strong bond he'd established with his grandfather. Rags, of course, was another reason, but Vienna soon found herself thinking that if Drew was to spend time with his son and show him that he cared, Chris would happily go anywhere with him.

"That was delicious," Vienna declared a little later, as she placed her knife and fork on the empty plate. "But I think I ate too much."

She sighed and leaned back in her chair, brushing a few bread crumbs from her navy skirt. The calf-length full skirt was one of her favorites and she was glad she'd chosen to wear it tonight, along with her white silk blouse.

It was hard to believe that Christmas was practically upon them. As yet she'd done nothing in preparation. By now, Tobias would have bought a Christmas tree from one of the Christmas-tree lots in town, and she, in turn, would have brought down the decorations stored in the attic.

Her eyes came to rest on the baubles and lights on the tree in the foyer of the restaurant, and suddenly an idea formed in her mind. Surely Drew wouldn't be able to resist the pull of Christmas and all that went with it? If she could convince him to take Chris to the Christmas tree-lot so they could choose a tree together, perhaps after dinner they could all decorate it. It was worth a try. And if it helped to build a closer bond between Drew and his son, so much the better. This thought made her smile.

"It's time for a toast." Drew's voice cut into her meandering thoughts. She turned to him, filled with a sense of purpose.

"What's a toast?" Chris asked. "Is it dessert?"

Vienna couldn't stifle the laughter that bubbled to the surface.

"No, not quite," Drew replied, laughter in his voice, too. "We raise our glasses and wish Vienna a happy birthday," he explained.

"But aren't we going to have a birthday cake?" Chris insisted.

"First things first," said Drew, smiling now. "Just follow my lead," he added as he raised his wineglass.

Vienna lifted her glass and Drew touched it with his. Chris quickly joined in, knocking his tall glass—none too gently—against theirs.

"Easy," Drew cautioned. Then, glancing across at Vienna, he smiled. "Happy Birthday."

"Happy Birthday," echoed Chris.

Over the rim of her glass Vienna again noticed laughter lurking in the depths of Drew's eyes, and a shiver of awareness chased along her nerve endings.

When Drew smiled like that she saw the warmth, the caring that had always been such an integral part of the man she'd known. Glimpsing it again reminded her of the young man she'd been close to falling in love with the night of her sixteenth birthday—the night he'd danced with her in the orchard.

Just for a moment that hard edge, that protective shield he'd built around himself vanished, allowing her to see the vulnerability and the pain he worked hard to keep hidden. Intuitively, she sensed that the resemblance between Drew and his son was more than just physical; emotionally, they were alike, too. They'd both been hurt by Natalie, and that pain ran deep; but more significant, they were both afraid to care, afraid to love.

"Here's the cake!" Chris almost shouted as the waitress arrived at the table with a small chocolate birthday cake, complete with candles.

Chris eagerly helped Vienna blow out the candles. When the cake was cut and served and the waitress had departed, Drew leaned toward his son. "Do you think you'll be all right on your own for a few minutes, Chris?" he asked in a conspiratorial tone.

"Sure, but why?" Chris asked.

Drew leaned closer and whispered in the boy's ear. Vienna watched as Chris grinned at her, then at his father before turning his attention to the piece of cake on the plate in front of him.

"Come on, Vienna," coaxed Drew. "I told Chris that we both need to take a turn around the dance-floor in order to make room for that birthday cake."

She started to protest, but Drew was already on his feet. With his hand at her elbow, he ushered her toward the dancefloor. The band was playing a slow, romantic ballad, and when Drew pulled her gently into his arms, Vienna closed her eyes and began to dream.

The music floated around them and somehow she managed to make her feet follow Drew's. But all the while she was conscious only of the man holding her, and the memory of another birthday and a cold winter night so long ago.

She had thought she was in heaven then; but it was nothing compared to what she was feeling now. With his lean body pressed firmly against hers, she felt a strange new longing. And as she breathed in the rich masculine scent of his spicy cologne and felt the smooth fabric of his jacket against her cheek, it was all she could do to stop herself from turning her head a little and finding his mouth with her own.

She'd never known that simply dancing with a man could elicit such a feeling of utter contentment. It felt so right to be in his arms, as if somehow a part of her had been missing and now for the first time she felt whole. What was happening to her? What was this overwhelming emotion that had curled around her heart and captured her very soul?

"You can blame Tobias for this." Drew spoke the words softly into her ear.

Vienna took a steadying breath, and drawing away, she looked up at him. "Tobias?"

"He told me that if I brought you here, I had to be sure to dance one dance," he explained.

"Oh . . ." she said, and at his words, the peace and joy she'd been experiencing only moments ago vanished like a puff of smoke. She felt the blood drain from her face. Drew hadn't wanted to dance with her—he was only doing this because Tobias had suggested it.

"I know that I'm merely filling in for your friend Bruce, tonight," she heard Drew say. "Word has it he's been accepted onto the hospital board. Next he'll be looking for a suitable wife. I assume you must be in the running." The words were spoken in a detached, almost cynical tone that made her stiffen in anger.

"Actually, he's already proposed," Vienna said with a false brightness, and was immediately annoyed with herself for thinking that her words would hurt him.

"My, my," was his soft reply. "And have you accepted?" he asked in that infuriatingly calm voice.

She swallowed convulsively. "I'm still thinking about it," she managed, thankful that she, too, sounded calm and in control.

Drew made no comment and when the music stopped a few moments later, he released her immediately.

When they returned to the table, she busied herself talking to Chris while Drew attended to the bill. She even managed to eat a few bites of the chocolate cake set before her, but all the while she was conscious of Drew's silence and the dark, brooding expression on his face.

"Do you want to drop in at the hospital and see Tobias before we go home?" he asked as they made their way from the restaurant.

"Won't he be asleep?" In truth she didn't feel up to facing Tobias. He would know instantly that something had upset her, and she didn't want him worrying about her on top of everything else.

"You're probably right," Drew agreed as he started the engine.

"We can tell Gramps all about it tomorrow," suggested Chris.

It wasn't long before Chris fell asleep in the back seat, and feeling disinclined to talk, Vienna was relieved that Drew, too, seemed content to remain silent. Throughout the drive home, she thought about those moments on the dancefloor when Drew had commented about Bruce. She knew she'd given him the impression that she was indeed seriously considering Bruce's proposal, and now she wished she hadn't let herself react in that way.

By the time Drew brought the wagon to a halt outside the house, her thoughts had turned to Chris and just how she was going to approach Drew and suggest that he spend more time with the boy.

"Thank you for a wonderful dinner, Drew," she said politely as he brought the wagon to a halt in front of the house.

"My pleasure," he replied, but his tone lacked warmth.

"Chris enjoyed himself, too, I think," Vienna said a few minutes later as she held the kitchen door open for Drew, who had carried the sleeping child from the car.

"Looks that way," Drew commented. "If you'll excuse me, I'll just take him upstairs and put him right to bed. Good night," he added, leaving her alone in the kitchen.

Vienna let the dogs out for a final run and as she stood staring up at the stars, she decided that the time to put forward her idea was now while she still had the courage, and while Chris was asleep.

When the dogs returned, she settled them once more. Then, with a fleeting glance at the carnations in the vase on the kitchen table, she made her way upstairs.

It came as no surprise to see that the light in Tobias's office was on. She crossed to the door, and taking a deep breath, tapped softly and entered.

Drew looked up from the papers on the desk, and she saw a questioning look come into his eyes.

"I'd like to talk to you about Chris," she said.

"Chris? Is there a problem I'm not aware of?" Drew asked coolly.

She bit back a sigh. "Christmas is a very important time for children," she began tentatively. "I'm sure you remember the anticipation and excitement you felt when you were seven." She paused and met his gaze, but there was no encouragement in his eyes. She thought of Chris and forged on. "With all that's been going on around here, Christmas seems to have been forgotten, and I thought it might be a good idea if you were to take Chris into town, go shopping with him, or just take him to see Santa. It would give you a chance to get to know him better, to find out what it is he's hoping Santa will bring him. You can even help him choose a present for Tobias. And then, of course, there's the job of picking out a tree."

She knew she was rambling, but she couldn't seem to stop. "While you're out I could get the decorations down from the attic and then the two of you could decorate the tree together...." Her voice trailed off when she saw Drew's jaw tighten and the expression in his eyes change to barely suppressed anger.

"Are you trying to tell me I don't spend enough time with Chris?" he asked, pushing away from the desk and getting to his feet.

"No...yes... I mean, I just thought..." She tripped over the words, all the while aware that he was coming around the desk toward her.

"That's exactly what you're saying, Vienna," he told her pointedly.

"Chris is only seven, Drew. He needs to know that you care about him," she said, and immediately regretted her choice of words. He stopped in front of her and she could feel his anger coming at her in waves. She was tempted to take a step back, but she held her ground.

"I do care about my son. I care about him very much," insisted Drew, emotion edging into his voice now.

"Then show him," Vienna blurted out.

"Dammit, Vienna, I've tried." He ran a hand through his hair in a gesture of despair.

"Then you'll just have to try harder," she said softly, hoping to ease the pain her words might cause. "Have you thought about this from his point of view? His mother dies, and suddenly Chris finds himself with a father he's never known about or seen before. I don't know what kind of mother Natalie was, Drew, but I'd guess she wasn't the best. Sometimes when I'm with Chris I see and hear a little of what I was like myself as a child, before you and your father came into my life and taught me about family, about— love." She stopped, her throat clogging with emotion now. She glanced at Drew, expecting him to rain a torrent of anger on her. Instead, his face was both thoughtful and bemused; and with that look, he stole another piece of her heart.

She took a steadying breath and continued. "Chris is a Sheridan—stubborn and proud, just like his father and grandfather before him. Don't you see that? But he's afraid to trust you, and you really can't blame him. How does he know that you won't be like his mother and leave him? How does he know he can trust you, when you're not prepared to spend some time with him, showing him that you love him. Oh, I know you've tried, but most of the time you're shut up in this room. Chris wants to trust you, to love you—believe me," she said, a catch in her voice now. "But you have to earn that trust."

Vienna watched as Drew's jaw tightened and his eyes stared at her, unseeing. Suddenly she had the strongest urge to reach out and soothe away the tension on his face, to kiss away the lines of strain she could see near his strong mouth.

"Drew?" She spoke his name tentatively and her hand came up to touch him, an action that sent a jolt of awareness chasing along her arm.

"Why?" The word startled her, but before she could answer, Drew continued. "Why do you care so much, Vienna, about Chris...or for that matter, me?" His dark eyes held hers, and under their probing gaze she had to fight the emotions suddenly threatening to overwhelm her.

"Because..." She cleared her throat and tried again. "Chris is a little boy who's hurting inside. He wants to be loved, he wants to belong—" She stopped when Drew's hand came up to capture her chin.

"*I'm* not a little boy, Vienna." His voice was low and husky. "Shall I prove it to you?" he challenged, and before she could even think or breathe, his mouth came down on hers.

Fire swept through her, bringing with it an array of heart-stopping, nerve-shattering sensations that had her clinging to Drew, never wanting to let go.

His tongue slid between her teeth and entwined with hers in a slow erotic dance that startled her senses and aroused a need that was both alien and exciting. So this was desire—this ache deep inside her that only he could appease, this longing to give everything his kisses demanded, this overwhelming need to become a part of the man who had already stolen her heart.

Drew was the catalyst, the firebrand, the man who had burned down the walls of fear and resistance and uncovered the sensual woman within her, the woman she hadn't known she could be. But it was all for

Drew—only for Drew. And just as this realization began to slowly sink in, he suddenly thrust her from him and held her at arm's length.

"I must be insane," he said, grinding out the words in a voice that was full of self-loathing. His hands dropped away and she stumbled, but he made no move to steady her.

Bewildered beyond measure, Vienna raised her eyes to meet his and almost cried out when she saw the look of disappointment in their depths.

"I think you'd better go now," Drew told her, in a voice empty of emotion. "I'm not sure your future husband would approve—"

"Drew—"

"No more. I've had just about enough for one night." With that, he turned and crossed to the window, where he stood looking out over the orchards.

A sob rose in her throat, but she fought it back. Gathering her tattered emotions, Vienna left the room.

Chapter Nine

Tears trickled unheeded down Vienna's face as she undressed and climbed into bed. She could still see the look of loathing in Drew's eyes, and she knew that the memory of that moment would stay with her forever.

Why had she pretended she was seriously considering marriage to Bruce?

From the moment Drew arrived on the doorstep she'd been fighting her true feelings for him. Seeing him again, having him near, had reawakened emotions she'd kept hidden in a special corner of her heart.

She was in love with Drew—deeply, irrevocably in love with him. And she realized with startling insight that her love had simply lain dormant over the years; that she'd been waiting, hoping and praying he would one day return.

The first time she'd been aware of her feelings for Drew had been the night of her sixteenth birthday, when he'd pulled her into his arms and danced with her in the orchard. Though the emotions he'd aroused then had frightened and bewildered her, somehow she'd known that Drew was the only man she would ever love.

She'd prided herself at being able to keep her feelings hidden, but Natalie had seen and recognized the change in her and had taken a perverse pleasure, whenever they were alone, in teasing Vienna.

She'd died a thousand deaths wondering if Natalie had told Drew how she felt, but when he continued to treat her as he always had, she'd hugged her secret to herself and dreamed that one day...

Vienna vividly remembered the fight that had erupted between Drew and his father, and the angry words they'd hurled at each other. She could still see the smug, self-satisfied look on Natalie's face as she and Drew had climbed into the car and driven away.

Though she'd been aware of a deep pain in her heart as she watched Drew leave, Vienna's primary concern had been Tobias. His anger had lasted for days, and as the days stretched into weeks, it had gradually turned to pain, and bewilderment, and finally—a profound sadness.

But Drew had suffered, too, thought Vienna as she recalled his brief but telling revelation about his marriage to Natalie. The bitterness and distrust that surrounded him had been Natalie's doing, but Drew's own pride and stubbornness had prevented him from returning after the failure of his marriage. And even after eight years, he persisted in being stubborn, determined to cling to the independence for which he'd paid such a high price. Vienna wondered if Drew realized that unless he was willing to let go of the past and trust in the future, he was in danger of losing so much more—his son.

Vienna spent a restless night. By six o'clock, she decided there was little point in trying to sleep any longer, and she rose and dressed in jeans and a warm sweater. She tiptoed downstairs and after fussing with the dogs, she let them outside, where a fresh layer of snow covered the ground.

She busied herself making banana bran muffins, and when they were in the oven she filled the coffeepot. Not for the first time that morning, she found her thoughts turning to Drew and their encounter in Tobias's office.

She'd spoken up purely for Chris's sake, but she wasn't at all sure Drew would even consider her suggestions. Still, she didn't regret trying. If she regretted anything, it was the wanton way she'd responded to his devastating kiss.

"Morning, Vienna." Chris's voice startled her out of her daydream. She turned from the stove to smile at him, inwardly relieved that he'd come downstairs before his father.

"Good morning," she said, and immediately noticed the happy expression on the boy's face.

"Dad says we're going to the mall today, after we visit Gramps. He's taking me to see Santa, and then we're going to do some Christmas shopping," announced Chris, his eyes sparkling with excitement.

"That's great!" She could scarcely believe what she'd heard. Drew had listened, after all! A warm glow of happiness settled around her heart.

"Mmm...Something smells good," Chris said.

At that moment, the stovetimer began to buzz. Picking up the oven gloves, Vienna retrieved the muffin trays and carried them to the counter.

"Is that freshly baked muffins I smell?" It was Drew who spoke and Vienna glanced up in time to see him enter the kitchen.

He wore gray pants and a black-and-gray patterned sweater, and he looked incredibly attractive. Her heart began to hammer wildly as their eyes met, and that familiar shiver of response danced across her skin.

"Freshly baked muffins it is," she said, and turned her attention back to the task in hand, acutely aware of Drew's eyes watching her every move.

Crossing to the table, she set the plate of muffins in the middle and lifted her gaze to meet his once more.

"Coffee?" she asked, a slight tremor in her voice.

"I'll get it," Drew said. He moved toward the coffeepot on the stove, brushing by her to reach it. At their brief contact, Vienna felt as if she'd been jolted by a live electric wire.

She heard Drew mutter under his breath, but she was too preoccupied trying to control her own response to register what he had said.

Chris reached for a muffin and so did Vienna, all the while hating herself for reacting at all. It was thanks to Chris's continuous chatter about the upcoming expedition to the mall that she managed to make it through the remainder of the meal.

She pinned a smile on her face and listened as Drew patiently answered Chris's questions about the stores they would visit. But not once did Drew address her or include her.

"You're coming with us, aren't you, Vienna?" Chris asked, as if he'd suddenly realized she hadn't been contributing to the conversation.

"Actually, I have some paperwork that needs taking care of at the clinic," she said easily. "You can drop me off there first, and pick me up later," she added, careful to avoid Drew's gaze.

"But I thought you didn't usually work on Saturdays," Chris said.

"Sometimes I have to," replied Vienna.

"Chris," Drew said in a cautionary tone, "if Vienna wants us to drop her at the clinic, that's exactly what we'll do." His voice was firm and matter-of-fact, but Vienna heard the underlying edge. He didn't want her with them. It was as simple as that. But even though she understood that he was taking her advice about spending time alone with Chris, she couldn't help feeling disappointed.

"Let's clean up, and then we can get this show on the road," Drew continued, and at his words, Chris jumped down from his chair and began to carry dishes to the sink.

"Aren't you coming with us to see Gramps?" Chris asked a while later when Drew brought the wagon to a halt outside the clinic.

"Tell him I'll walk over later," answered Vienna as she climbed out.

"Give Rags a hug for me," said Chris. "Tell him I'll play with him when we come back."

"I will. Have a good time." Vienna waved as they drove away.

She unlocked the clinic door and went inside, annoyed at the feeling of loneliness that suddenly descended upon her. She let Rags out and he danced around her feet, wagging his tail with unbridled pleasure at the sight of her. "At least *you*'re glad to see me," Vienna told him, then silently scolded herself for indulging in self-pity. Slipping a leash on Rags, she led him outside.

When she returned a few minutes later, the telephone was ringing.

"Forrester Veterinary Clinic, Dr. Forrester speaking," she said.

"Is your clinic open this morning?" an anxious voice asked, and Vienna immediately recognized Donna Whitehead, the wife of a local merchant and a longstanding member of the community.

"Yes," she answered.

"Thank goodness," was the reply. "This is Donna Whitehead. Samson is ill. He's been coughing all night and now he's just lying there, listless and he won't eat."

"Bring him right in," instructed Vienna, and frowned as she replaced the receiver. Donna was one of a group of residents who, ever since Vienna's run-in with Olivia Harvey-Smythe four months ago, had stopped bringing their pets to her clinic.

The fact that she was bringing Samson to Vienna now seemed unusual, to say the least, but there was little point in wasting time trying to guess at the reason.

While she waited for Donna to arrive, Vienna put Rags back into his cage, then returned to her office and tried to concentrate on the paperwork on her desk. During the past week, business had picked up—but not enough to shift the red figures on her balance sheet into the black, she thought with a frustrated sigh.

She'd bought the clinic with money she'd inherited from her father. The small amount she'd had left was disappearing now, too, thanks to the obligations she had to meet each month.

"Trying to balance the books?"

Vienna glanced up to find Sara and Tim standing in the doorway.

"Trying," said Vienna, with a weak smile.

"Is Chris around?" Sara asked. "Tim thought he might like to come Christmas shopping with us."

"He's gone shopping with his father," Vienna told them.

"Is he going to the mall to see Santa?" asked Tim.

"Yes," she replied, smiling.

"Why didn't you go with them?" Sara asked.

"Oh, I wanted to catch up on this paperwork," Vienna said easily. "And it's just as well, because Donna Whitehead telephoned to ask if she could bring Samson in."

"Mrs. Whitehead is bringing Samson here?" Sara said in a surprised voice. "Well, well. That's a turnaround. Maybe this business with Rags has finally shown people around here that Mrs. Harvey-Smythe is nothing but a pompous—"

"Sara, don't—" Vienna cut in quickly, but before she could say more, the outer door opened and Donna Whitehead entered. Behind her came her teenage son, Mike, and in his arms he carried Samson, a rather dejected-looking springer spaniel.

"Want me to stay?" Sarah whispered as Vienna moved to open the door to one of the examination rooms.

"Right in here, Mike," said Vienna. Over her shoulder, she answered Sara, "Thanks, but I'll manage."

"It's so good of you to see Samson," Donna said as she followed Vienna into the examination room.

"Not at all," Vienna said.

After a thorough examination, it was evident to Vienna that Samson was suffering from pneumonia. She learned that the dog had fallen through the ice at a pond on the farm, and though he'd been hauled out and dried off fairly quickly, he'd obviously been in the frigid water much too long.

Vienna administered an antibiotic and explained to Donna that although pneumonia was difficult to treat in dogs, she was hopeful that Samson would respond well to the medication.

Mike carried Samson out to the car, but Donna lingered. "Did you hear that Olivia Harvey-Smythe is selling Hillcrest and moving to Ontario?" the woman asked.

"No . . . I didn't," Vienna replied, trying with difficulty to hide the surprise she felt.

"Jean Kane down at the real estate office told me yesterday," Donna said. "She also told me Olivia wanted you to destroy that beautiful purebred retriever of hers, the one Sam Williamson found injured on the road."

"Olivia was very upset when she heard about Rags. She thought he'd been badly mauled, just like Brigadoon," Vienna explained, not altogether sure why she was jumping to the defense of the woman who was the cause of her problems at the clinic.

"But I understood she didn't want him because he's badly scarred," Donna went on.

"That's true, but—" Vienna began.

"How anyone could just give up an animal like that, I simply don't understand. It made me stop and think," Donna said, meeting Vienna's eyes with a penetrating gaze. "Well, I'll bring Samson back in a day or two, and you can check him over."

"Fine," Vienna agreed, and with a wave, Donna was gone.

Vienna closed the door and returned to her office, quietly contemplating the news about Olivia Harvey-Smythe. Though she wasn't sorry to hear that Olivia would be leaving Peachville, Vienna couldn't help wishing she'd been on better terms with the dog breeder.

Samson was only one of several patients Vienna treated during the course of the morning. She couldn't recall a Saturday when she'd been busier, and by early afternoon she was feeling a warm glow of satisfaction as well as a resurgence of hope that the future of the clinic was no longer quite so bleak.

Taking a much-needed break, Vienna walked to the delicatessen on the corner and ordered a sandwich and coffee. When she finished eating, she completed the short distance to the hospital, her thoughts on Chris and Drew, wondering how their shopping expedition was going.

"It's about time you showed up," Tobias said, patting the space on the bed beside him. "Sit here and tell me all about your birthday dinner. Chris seemed to think you had a good time, but that son of mine didn't say too much about anything this morning."

"Dinner was lovely, Tobias," Vienna told him with a smile. "But we missed you." She leaned over to kiss his leathery cheek.

"I'm sorry I wasn't there," said Tobias, a catch in his voice. "I'll make it up to you when I get out of this darned place," he added gruffly.

"The best present you could give me is to get well and come home."

"Nobody wants that more than I do." Tobias sighed with impatience. "I hate sitting around here doing nothing, especially when there are a few things that need my attention...."

"Just tell me what they are and I'll do them," Vienna offered.

"No...no, that's all right," said Tobias, sounding a little flustered.

"Perhaps Drew could help," Vienna suggested. "Why don't you ask him?"

"Ha! And wouldn't he like that," Tobias scoffed. "It's none of his business, and if he thinks he can come waltzing back here and take over—"

Tobias's hands started to shake and a vein throbbed at his temple. Vienna immediately regretted her impulse to try to coax Tobias into telling her about his problems.

"Don't! You're only upsetting yourself," she said, concern in her voice. "Let's talk about something else... Let's talk about when the doctor thinks you'll be able to come home."

Tobias took several steadying breaths and managed a weak smile before he spoke. "Next week, I hope. Just in time for Christmas. And believe me, it's not a moment too soon," he added, and again Vienna saw a look of worry come into his eyes.

Suddenly, there was a soft tap on the door and a nurse joined them.

"Time for your medication, Mr. Sheridan," the nurse announced brightly. "And then it's time for your nap."

"I'd better get back to the clinic in case Drew and Chris are waiting for me," Vienna said, rising from the bed. She bent toward Tobias and kissed him once more. "See you tomorrow. And try not to worry."

Dark clouds filled with the promise of snow were gathering in the sky as Vienna made the journey back to the clinic. The storm that had been predicted on the radio that morning seemed about to materialize she thought, as she reached the back door of the clinic.

All was quiet inside and there was no sign of the station wagon. Vienna decided to take Rags for a much-needed walk. As she returned to the parking lot at the rear of the building, the car came around the corner.

At the sight of a fir tree tied securely to the wagon's roofrack, Vienna smiled. The moment the car stopped, the passenger door was flung open and Chris came bounding toward her, his eyes alight with joy and laughter.

Rags barked and tugged at the leash, eager to welcome his friend.

"Vienna, we got a Christmas tree! My dad let me pick it out all by myself," Chris informed her proudly as he bent to hug Rags, and Vienna had to fight to swallow the lump of emotion suddenly trapped in her throat.

"It looks great, Chris," she said. "Seems to me that you had fun today." Her glance strayed to the tall figure who'd emerged from the driver's side of the car. Her heart flipped over at the sight of Drew's warm, welcoming smile.

"We did have fun, didn't we, son?" said Drew as he came around to join them.

"Yeah!" Chris smiled up at his father. "First we went to see Gramps, then we went to the mall. There was a big line to see Santa, but we waited and shared a bag of popcorn till it was my turn."

"And did you tell Santa what you wanted for Christmas?" Vienna asked, casting a brief glance at Drew.

"Yes, but it's a secret, 'cause if I tell you, then Santa won't bring it," Chris explained in a serious tone.

"Oh, I see," said Vienna. She tried not to laugh when she caught sight of Drew's expression, which told her all too clearly that he had no idea what his son wanted for Christmas.

"Then what did you do?" Vienna continued as she unlocked the door to the clinic.

Chris and Rags slid past her and she followed them inside. Drew brought up the rear.

"Then we looked through all the stores," Chris went on. "And we picked out a present for Gramps, and a present for you—" He stopped abruptly and flashed a guilty look at his father. "Sorry, Dad. I forgot."

"That's all right," said Drew, gently ruffling his son's hair. "You didn't tell her what the present was, and she'll never guess, right?"

"Right." Chris grinned conspiratorially, and the look that passed between father and son warmed Vienna's heart.

"Are you all through here?" Drew asked.

"Yes," said Vienna. "I just have to put Rags in his cage. Come on, boy."

"Wait," Drew said, causing both Chris and Vienna to turn to him in surprise. "Now that he's recovering, I can see that it's not fair to shut him up in a cage all night. If you want to bring Rags back to the house, it's fine with me."

"Do you mean it, Dad?" Chris asked, his voice little more than a whisper.

Drew nodded, but his expression became serious and he crouched down to the boy's level. "As long as you understand, Chris, that I haven't had a change of heart. Rags is Vienna's responsibility and she'll still be looking for a new home for him."

"I understand," Chris answered solemnly, seconds before he buried his face in Rags's neck. "You're coming home with us, Rags!"

Throughout the drive home Chris, with Rags contentedly riding beside him in the back seat, chattered about the events of the day. By the time they reached the house, it was snowing heavily.

There was considerable commotion in the kitchen as Buffy and Daisy were introduced to Rags, but wagging tails and friendly greetings prevailed.

"We'll need the Christmas-tree stand," Drew said when he joined them in the kitchen.

"And the decorations," Chris piped up from his seat on the floor with the dogs.

"Everything is in the attic," Vienna told them. "I'll get the stand down first—you two bring in the tree."

Vienna ran upstairs and pulled down the ladder that led to the attic. She quickly climbed the steps to the storage area and found the stand, as well as a number of boxes marked Christmas Decorations. She hurried back downstairs in time to hold the door open for Drew, Chris, and the Christmas tree.

After much straining, groaning and panting, the tree was carried into the living room and secured in the stand. As they stood back to admire it, Vienna collided with the coffee table and stumbled against Drew.

"Careful," he warned as his hands came up to steady her. Her face was only scant inches from his and she could smell the fragrance of fir and earth that clung to him. Her heart began to react to his nearness the way it always did—beating madly against her rib cage as though it were trying to escape.

When she lifted her eyes to meet his, she saw a flash of emotion in their dark depths, but it was gone before she could even begin to decipher it.

For what seemed like an eternity, they stood gazing at each other, trapped in an endless moment. Then Vienna felt herself begin to sway toward him—whether at his urging or of her own volition, she wasn't sure. All she knew was the need to feel his mouth on hers.

"Are we going to decorate the tree now?" Chris spoke up from behind them.

Drew's hands instantly dropped away and he took a step back. "The decorations are in the attic. Come and give me a hand to get them down," he said, already moving toward the door. With a fleeting smile for Vienna, Chris ran after his father.

Vienna released the breath she'd been holding and willed her heart to slow its frantic pounding. Drew had been about to kiss her, she'd been sure of it. Then, suddenly, his expression had changed and a look of intense anger had darkened his eyes.

The look had held the power of a physical blow. Feeling bruised and more than a little vulnerable, Vienna retreated to the kitchen. Somehow she sensed that she was responsible for the change in Drew, and now she was unwilling to face him.

"Want to help us decorate the tree?" Chris popped his head around the corner. Vienna glanced at the boy and saw the look of anticipation and excitement in his eyes.

"You go ahead," she said. "I'll inspect it when you're done."

"Okay," Chris said and disappeared.

For the next hour Vienna busied herself making lemon chicken. She'd deliberately picked that recipe because she was unfamiliar with it and she knew it would keep her busy in the kitchen for quite a while.

But as the sounds of low voices and laughter drifted to her from the living room, she began to wish she'd accepted Chris's invitation to help trim the tree.

She was putting the finishing touches on the salad when she heard Chris's voice behind her.

"We're finished, Vienna," he announced. "Want to come and inspect it now?"

"Of course." Wiping her hands on a tea towel, she followed Chris into the living room.

The tree stood in the big bay window, its lights twinkling a welcome. At the sight of it, in all its finery, Vienna's eyes filled with tears.

"It's perfect." She could hardly get the words past the lump in her throat. "You've both done a wonderful job." She smiled down at Chris, whose face was beaming with pride.

"Dad strung the lights and I hung most of the other decorations," he informed her. "We found some neat ornaments, like the tiny wooden Santa and a set of reindeer." He moved to the tree to point them out to her. "Dad says he remembers them from when he was a kid like me," Chris explained.

Vienna glanced at Drew, who'd been standing near the fireplace watching and listening. She'd been aware of him from the moment she entered the room, and it had taken all her willpower not to look at him.

"Tobias got them from an old man who came to the door one Christmas selling his wares," Drew told them, the low timbre of his voice sending a shiver down her spine. "I remember he had a wagon full of carvings of every shape, size and description, but I liked Santa and the reindeer best and I said so. I didn't know until Christmas morning that Tobias had bought them for me. I remember coming downstairs and there they were, hanging on the tree."

"They're really neat." Chris gently touched the small wooden Santa.

Vienna opened her mouth to say something, but no words came. She cleared her throat, trying to hide the fact that Drew's story had affected her. "You and your dad have done a great job, Chris. I've never seen a more beautifully decorated tree," she managed at last.

Chris beamed with obvious delight and Vienna found herself smiling back, but she avoided looking at Drew. Boxes and papers were strewn about and she began to gather some of the empty boxes.

"You must both be hungry. Dinner's almost ready," Vienna said. "Why don't you go and wash up first?"

"Okay," said Chris, and with one last glance at the tree in the window, he scampered off.

"I'll clean this up later," said Vienna suddenly realizing that she was alone with Drew. She moved to follow Chris, but she'd only taken one step when Drew spoke.

"Vienna, wait. There's something I need to say." She turned to look at him. "I thought a lot about what you said last night and I decided you were right, that I had been neglecting Chris. So I took your advice, and frankly I'm amazed at the results. Chris and I had a great day together. I learned a lot about my son—we *both* learned a lot—and I want to thank you.''

Vienna fought down the emotions threatening to overwhelm her. ''I'm glad I could help,'' she said, her voice trembling.

Drew seemed about to say more, but Chris came clattering down the stairs and into the living room. Vienna wasn't sure whether or not she was glad of the intrusion this time, but Chris's presence somehow helped to ease the tension that had once again sprung up between her and Drew.

The meal she'd toiled over was well received. When they were finished eating, Chris and Drew helped clear away the dishes while Vienna made hot chocolate.

Outside, large white featherlike flakes dropped in seemingly endless succession from the sky. Drew said something about lighting a fire in the living room fireplace. Chris eagerly offered to help and followed his father from the room.

A few minutes later, carrying a tray with three mugs of hot chocolate, Vienna returned to the living room. Drew and Chris had tidied away the empty boxes and lit a fire. The red, green and yellow lights on the Christmas tree and the glow from the fire gave the room a warm ambience that had chased away all the earlier tensions.

Vienna sat down in the big old armchair by the fire and with a tired sigh, relaxed against the cushions. It wasn't long before she began to hum a Christmas carol.

''Why don't you play that on the piano, Vienna?'' Drew asked.

"Is my singing that bad?" She smiled across at Drew in the soft light.

"Your singing is fine," Drew replied, a rumble of laughter in his voice. "But I haven't heard you play for a long time."

"Can you play?" Chris set his mug on the table and gazed eagerly at her.

"I'm a little rusty—I haven't played for ages," she told him.

"Aw—please?" Chris pleaded, already halfway to the upright piano on the other side of the fireplace.

"If you look inside the piano bench, you'll find some music," Vienna told him, rising reluctantly to her feet.

Chris opened the bench, and together they rummaged through the music until they found several books of Christmas carols.

Vienna switched on the lamp nearby. Tentatively at first, she began to pick her way through the notes of a familiar carol. It wasn't long before Drew joined them at the piano. As his rich baritone voice floated around her, Vienna tried to ignore the way her body reacted to the seductive sound.

They were too busy singing to notice that the dogs had crept into the living room and were listening to the impromptu concert. Only when Rags suddenly began to howl along with them did Vienna stop in surprise.

"Rags is trying to sing, too," Chris said, hopping down from the piano bench and crossing to where Rags sat on the rug.

Vienna and Drew exchanged glances. At the laughter dancing in his eyes, her breath caught in her throat, and her heart went into a tailspin. She dropped her gaze, afraid he might see written on her face the depth of her feelings for him.

"Rags has quite a talent," Drew commented, as he moved to where Chris sat hugging the dog.

"He's the neatest dog in the whole world," said Chris emphatically. There was no mistaking the love in his voice, and in that instant Vienna knew exactly what Chris had asked Santa to bring him for Christmas. Her glance flew to Drew, but she could see nothing in his expression that indicated that he, too, had seen and understood.

"Time for bed, Chris," she heard Drew say.

"Can't I stay up a little longer?" Chris asked, even as he tried to stifle a yawn.

"You're almost asleep now," Drew pointed out with a smile.

"Please?" Chris gazed pleadingly at his father.

"Come on. I'll read you a story from one of those books we bought today," coaxed Drew, extending his hand in invitation.

"Okay." Giving Rags another hug, Chris stood. "Night, Rags, night, Vienna," he said as he placed his small hand in Drew's.

"Good night," said Vienna softly, and as she watched their retreating figures, an ache of longing tugged at her heart.

Chapter Ten

Vienna stood at the stove stirring a pot of porridge. It was Monday morning and as yet, neither Drew nor Chris had put in an appearance.

When she'd passed by Tobias's office on her way downstairs, she'd heard the low rumble of Drew's voice as he talked on the telephone.

Sighing, she let her gaze drift outside to the huge snowman standing like a sentinel amid the fruit trees in the backyard. They'd spent the best part of Sunday morning building him. Vienna smiled when she thought of the way Drew had thrown himself into the task of rolling the snow into what Chris had laughingly described as the world's largest snowball.

The entire day had been like something out of a dream. She couldn't recall a time when she'd had so much fun, and there had been moments when she'd found herself wishing the day could last forever.

It had been heartwarming to watch the relationship between Drew and Chris grow stronger by the minute, and the memory of their shared laughter at the height of an intense snowball fight, would, she knew, stay with her always.

They'd been like a family—husband, wife and child—and throughout the day Vienna had had to constantly remind herself that she was simply indulging in wishful thinking.

She'd been tempted all day to tell Drew that she wasn't considering Bruce's proposal of marriage at all, but somehow the opportunity never presented itself. And even if she told Drew, she wasn't sure it would make any difference.

"Morning, Vienna," said Chris. "Whatcha cooking?" He tried to peer into the pot she was stirring.

"Porridge," she told him, and smiled when she saw him wrinkle his nose.

"I don't think I like porridge," said Chris.

"Have you tasted it before?" she asked.

"No, but—" he began.

"Then why don't you try it?" she coaxed gently.

"Porridge tastes good when you sprinkle brown sugar on top," Drew said as he came up behind them.

Vienna's heart skipped a beat at the sound of his voice so close to her ear. She shut her eyes for a brief second in an attempt to control her reaction. Instead, her head filled with the fragrance of spice and leather as his dark, masculine scent stirred her senses and aroused faint tremors somewhere deep inside her.

"I'll have a bowl, please," Drew said as he picked up the coffeepot from the stove.

With a concentrated effort, Vienna managed to comply with Drew's request, but as she set the bowl in front of him, her hand trembled a little.

"Me too, please." Chris hopped onto the seat next to his father, watching with interest as Drew sprinkled rich, dark brown sugar over the porridge.

Vienna filled two more bowls, one for herself and one for Chris, and carried them to the table. Just as she was about to sit down, the telephone rang.

"I'll get it." Vienna crossed to the telephone on the wall next to the refrigerator and picked up the receiver. "Hello?"

"Hi!" a female voice greeted her cheerfully. "I'm Lana Montgomery. Is Drew there?"

"Just a moment, please," said Vienna politely. She turned to Drew. "It's Lana Montgomery."

Drew wiped his mouth with a napkin and rose from the table. As she handed him the receiver, their fingers touched for a fleeting moment, sending a jolt of awareness chasing along her arm. Vienna returned to the table and sat down, glad she had her back to Drew and that he hadn't noticed her reaction.

"Hi! I hoped it would be you," Drew began, his tone warm and affectionate. He was silent for a long moment as he listened to Lana. "That's great, I knew you could pull it off," he said a few moments later. "Write up a contract." He paused and listened again. "Yes, I'll do that," he said, then gave a low chuckle. "Thanks . . . bye." Drew hung up the phone and returned to the table, a smile of satisfaction on his face.

"That was Lana, my assistant," he explained. "You remember her, don't you, Chris?"

"Yeah. She's the pretty lady that works in your office."

Drew laughed. "Not only is she pretty, she's the best assistant I've ever had," he continued with unmistakable sincerity.

At his words, a pain twisted inside Vienna, and she instantly recognized it as jealousy. She stood up abruptly, taking the bowl of porridge she'd barely touched to the sink. How could she be jealous of a woman she didn't know and had never even seen? she asked herself angrily.

As Vienna rinsed the dish under the water, she recalled the genuine warmth and affection she'd heard in Drew's voice when he'd spoken to... Lana. Could it be that Drew and his assistant were more than friends? Pain throbbed at her temples now.

"That's the call I've been waiting for, Vienna," Drew said.

It took every ounce of her strength to turn and look at him. "It was?" She fought to keep the tremor from her voice.

"Yes," he answered. "But now comes the difficult part—convincing Tobias that what I have in mind is in his best interests."

"Don't you think he'll approve?" she asked.

"I'm not sure. I hope so," he said slowly. "I just have a hunch about this—"

"What exactly is your plan?" Vienna's curiosity was overriding everything else now.

Drew smiled and his eyes lit up with excitement. "A friend of mine in San Francisco owns a small beverage company that specializes in fruit drinks. He only started up a few years ago, but he's been doing an incredible business. It suddenly occurred to me that we could do something very similar here. If we could produce a natural fruit drink made from the peaches, pears, and cherries grown right here in the orchards, we could tap into the market at a local level first, and then expand."

"It sounds like a wonderful idea," Vienna said enthusiastically. "But what about—"

"A number of questions occurred to me, too," Drew quickly cut in. "That's when I decided to call Josh in San Francisco and ask him how he got started."

"What did he say?" she asked.

"Josh was terrific. He gave me a complete rundown of how his operation works, and he also told me exactly what we'd need to get started," said Drew. "That's when I got Lana involved. I've had her calling around making inquiries about leasing equipment. She's done a great job tracking down some of the things we'll need."

"But wait a minute, Drew." Vienna reined in her rising excitement. "Who's going to finance this? Your father certainly isn't in any position to do that."

"Don't worry about that for the moment." Drew brushed aside her question. "If Tobias approves of the idea, I'm willing to put up the financing and carry the project until it gets on its feet."

"But Drew, Tobias is never going to agree..." Vienna started to protest.

He quickly forestalled her. "I've thought about this from every angle, Vienna, and I'm going to suggest to my father that we form a partnership. I'll supply the financial backing and he'll supply the fruit. It's a fair enough bargain, and once we get into production I know we'll have a winner.''

Vienna wished she could feel as confident as Drew sounded. He'd obviously gone to a great deal of trouble exploring the options and the angles. She knew that Tobias had once dreamed of the day when he'd hand over the orchards and the business to Drew, but that had been a long time ago. What would he think of going into partnership with his son now?

"But the summer is still so far away," Vienna reminded him. "Won't that be a drawback?"

"Actually, no," Drew replied. "That will work for us, because the time between now and the height of the season will be well spent, believe me, in setting up the operation."

"But what about the bank loan?" Vienna asked, wanting to make sure that this important issue was not forgotten.

"That's been taken care of," Drew said easily.

"You mean you've paid it off already?" She stared at him in astonishment.

"Yes."

"Oh, Drew." Vienna's eyes stung with the threat of tears, and she blinked them away. "But why haven't you told Tobias?"

Drew sighed. "I wanted to, but every time I tried to steer the conversation in that direction, he changed the subject. I was hoping he'd talk to me, tell me what was happening...ask for my help." He ran a hand through his hair. "At any rate," he hurried on, "it isn't a worry anymore. All I have to do now is to put forward the proposal for a partnership and hope that he makes a decision based on rationale and not emotion.''

''When are you planning to talk to him?'' Vienna asked.

''The sooner, the better.'' Drew glanced at his watch. ''We should think about leaving. Come on, Chris, time to brush your teeth and get ready for school.''

''Drew, are you sure you don't want me to come with you?'' Vienna asked as he brought the station wagon to a halt outside the clinic an hour later.

''Thanks, Vienna, I appreciate all that you've done,'' Drew said. ''But this is between my father and me.''

''Call me and let me know what he says.'' Vienna couldn't help but admire his confidence. He was obviously a man used to negotiating business deals, and in that respect, this was certainly no different. But as she unlocked the back door of the clinic she said a silent prayer.

''I'll tell Tim we're here,'' said Chris, and ran toward the door that led to Sara's apartment.

The telephone rang as Vienna entered and she quickly went to answer it. When Sara, Tim and Chris joined her a few minutes later, she was smiling.

''All set?'' she asked the boys.

''Tim built a fort yesterday,'' Chris told her excitedly. ''We're going to play there later when we come back from school.''

"That sounds like fun," Vienna said.

"Time to go," said Sara. "See you both later. Come straight home," she reminded them, and with a wave they were gone.

"So, how was your weekend?" Sara asked, turning to Vienna.

"Nice," Vienna said. "Chris and Drew put up the Christmas tree and then decorated it."

"You really like him, don't you?" Sara commented, and at her words, Vienna felt a telltale blush begin to creep over her face.

"You mean Chris?" Vienna tried to keep her tone noncommittal.

"Yes," replied Sara.

"Oh...of course, he's a great kid," said Vienna, annoyed with herself for having misinterpreted the casual question.

"Drew's rather nice, too," Sara said, watching Vienna closely this time.

"Yes, he is," she answered. "Oh, by the way, Louella Campbell just called. She's bringing Princess in for her shots this morning." Vienna knew full well this information would distract Sara.

"Louella Campbell?" Sara repeated. "Well, all I can say is, it looks like people around here are finally coming to their senses. I'll never know why anyone paid any heed to that Harvey-Smythe woman to start with—spreading those lies about you being an incompetent vet. I'd have sued her for every penny...." Sara paused. "If the mayor's wife is bringing in her dog, then it's my guess that it won't be long before all her friends will follow suit."

Tempted though she was, Vienna refrained from mentioning the news about Olivia Harvey-Smythe. Sara would hear about it soon, no doubt.

Vienna glanced at her watch. "Mrs. Campbell will be here any minute. I'd better get everything ready."

"That sounds like a car now." she confirmed, then grinned at Vienna. "I knew everything would work out," she said, reaching for the door.

Vienna hoped Sara was right. The fact that Louella Campbell and Donna Whitehead had brought their dogs to the clinic was indeed a promising start. But much as the survival of her veterinary clinic was important to her, Vienna found her thoughts turning to Drew.

How had Tobias reacted to his proposal of a partnership? She tried to imagine what Tobias would say when he learned that the house and orchards were freed from the threat of foreclosure. Surely he'd be pleased and relieved that the worry was no longer hanging over him.

"Good morning, Dr. Forrester." Louella Campbell's voice cut through her wayward thoughts and Vienna turned to greet the mayor's wife.

"How nice to see you, Mrs. Campbell," Vienna said. "And you, too, Princess," she added, bending down to pat the basset hound that stood shivering with apprehension at her owner's feet. "Come on, girl. Up on the table where I can have a look at you." Vienna gently lifted the dog onto the examination table.

After Princess and Mrs. Campbell left, Vienna returned to her office where she tried to catch up on some reading. But for once the medical journals held

little appeal and she found her eyes continually straying to the clock on the wall. It was almost eleven and
though there had been a few distractions that morning—an injured bird, and a dog with a small abscess
on his front paw—there had been no word from Drew.

With each minute that passed, the hope that Tobias had agreed on a partnership with Drew was fad-
ing fast. Sara had slipped out to buy muffins to go
with their coffee, and when the telephone suddenly
rang, Vienna knew, before she reached for the receiver, that it was Drew.

"Vienna?" The low, husky sound of her name sent
a shiver chasing down her spine.

"Yes."

"The jury is in and the verdict is an unqualified
no," Drew stated in a voice that held more than a trace
of anger and bitterness. "I've already called the airport and Chris and I are booked on the three-thirty
flight back to San Francisco. I'm on my way to the
school now to pick him up."

A wave of pain washed over her at the thought of
Chris and Drew leaving. "Drew, don't do this," she
pleaded. "Tobias just needs more time to get used to
the idea, that's all." The silence at the other end of the
telephone line effectively told her the extent of Drew's
anger.

She heard him take a deep breath. "I'm sorry, Vienna, but I don't have any more time left," he replied
in a tight, controlled voice. "Shall I pick you up after
I get Chris?"

"No, there's something I have to do first," said Vienna. "I'll catch up with you at the house."

When Sara returned a few minutes later, she readily complied to Vienna's request to borrow her car.

"I'll bring it back later this afternoon," she told Sara. "I'm going to the hospital to see Tobias, then I'll be at the house if you need me."

During the short journey to the hospital, Vienna tried to sort out what she would say to Tobias. From the little Drew had told her, she was sure that it was simply Tobias's stubbornness and pride that had prevented him from agreeing to Drew's plan and accepting the partnership.

Tobias looked up when she entered the room, and for a fleeting moment she thought she saw a flicker of disappointment in his eyes.

"I know why you're here, Vienna," he began, his voice firm and unyielding. "But my mind is made up." There was a hint of defiance in his tone.

"I came by to tell you that Chris and Drew are leaving," she said softly, crossing to stand by his bedside. "They're flying back to San Francisco this afternoon." At her words, she saw the blood drain from Tobias's face, and a look of pain come into his eyes.

"If that's what he wants to do, I can't stop him," Tobias said, but there was a faint tremor in his voice now.

"I can't say that I blame Drew for leaving," Vienna said. "But is that really what you want, Tobias? Have you thought about the fact that you may never see your grandson again?"

Tobias glanced at her and she saw the tears that came into his eyes. Love and compassion flowed through her, and she reached out to take his hand in hers. "Don't you think it's time to forgive and forget the past? Chris needs you. Drew needs you. And you need both of them."

"Then why didn't he come back before?" asked Tobias in a voice edged with pain. "He only came back because he thought I was dying."

"Tobias, that isn't fair," Vienna chided gently. "Drew told me that when Natalie left him he wanted to come home...wanted to come back...but he couldn't. Don't you remember what you said to him? You yelled at him not to come crawling back here...." She swallowed. "Your son is a lot like you, Tobias—stubborn and proud." At her words, a look of pride flashed in the old man's eyes.

"But pride and stubbornness almost cost you your life," she continued, bringing his hand to her cheek. "Isn't it time you put them aside and opened your heart a little?"

Tobias was silent for a long moment. Vienna held her breath, silently praying that he would see the error of his ways.

When she couldn't stand the silence any longer, she spoke again. "Drew's offering you a partnership, Tobias. He's willing to meet you halfway, to take the risk. Why aren't you?"

"It's too late, that's why," Tobias blurted out. "Where was he all those years when I needed him? Tell me that."

"Tobias..." she groaned. Frustration, annoyance and defeat gathered in her throat, making her want to scream. "It's Christmas—a time for putting aside old hurts. You have a wonderful son, and a terrific grandchild. What more could a man ask for?''

"I know you mean well, child," Tobias said, tiredness evident in his tone now. "But it's too late."

Tears stung Vienna's eyes and she blinked them away. "It's never too late," she said, her voice barely a whisper. She hesitated. "You're tired. I'd better go. You're a stubborn old fool, Tobias Sheridan." She kissed his cheek. "But I love you."

Out in the hallway, Vienna leaned against the wall for support and fought back the tears threatening to overwhelm her. Why did he have to be so stubborn? Surely there was something she could do?

If Tobias wouldn't budge, perhaps she could talk to Drew and ask him to reconsider. She had to give it one more try.

Pushing herself away from the wall, she hurried toward the elevators, punching the Down button impatiently. When the doors slid open a few seconds later, she found herself face-to-face with Bruce.

"Hello, Vienna. I was hoping I'd catch you," said Bruce with a welcoming smile. "Sara told me I might find you here."

"I'm sorry, Bruce, I'm in a bit of a rush," she said, trying to go around him. He easily blocked her path, and as the elevator doors closed, Vienna bit back her frustration.

"What's your hurry? I thought we'd have lunch. I'll tell you about the seminar." Bruce put his hand on her elbow and ushered her toward a small waiting area near the bank of elevators.

"I can't right now," insisted Vienna, trying without success to free herself. "I really have to go."

"Is there an emergency at the clinic?" Bruce asked.

"No...it's nothing like that." She avoided his eyes.

"Then what's so important that it can't wait?"

Vienna hesitated, but only for a moment. "It's Drew, I have to talk to him," she answered.

"What about?" A puzzled frown appeared on Bruce's face.

"He's leaving and I have to stop him," Vienna said, a hint of desperation in her voice now. She'd glanced up at the clock above the nurses' station a moment ago and noticed it was twelve-fifteen. If she didn't hurry, there was a strong possibility she might miss them, that they might already be on their way to the airport.

"Why would you want to stop him?" Bruce asked. "Unless there's something going on here you're not telling me."

Vienna felt her face grow warm under his steady gaze. "There's nothing going on."

"Then why don't you want Drew to leave?"

"I don't know what you mean," Vienna said, but her tone lacked conviction.

Bruce stared at her for a long moment. "Ever since Drew Sheridan arrived, you've been on edge, and acting different," he said softly. "At first I just put it down to worrying about Tobias, but I see now that it's much more than that. You're in love with Drew Sheridan, aren't you?"

The question startled Vienna, and she gazed at Bruce in utter astonishment. Words of denial almost made it to her lips, but Bruce held up his hands.

"Don't deny it," he told her with a sigh. "I can see it in your eyes. It explains a number of things that have puzzled me about you."

"Bruce, I'm sorry," she said. "It was never my intention to hurt you, believe me."

"I know." Bruce smiled sadly at her. "I guess there's really nothing more to be said. If you want to catch Drew, you'd better get going."

For a moment, Vienna couldn't move. Though Drew's arrival and the feelings he aroused in her had shown her exactly where her heart lay, she hadn't wanted her relationship with Bruce to end this way. But it was too late for regrets.

The sound of the elevator doors sliding open caught her attention, and she glanced up at him. There was no bitterness in his eyes, no anger, and for that she was grateful. "I'm sorry," she murmured again before slipping past him and into the elevator.

As she made her way to the car, her thoughts drifted once more to Bruce. He'd been so kind, so understanding, that she almost wished she did love him. But love was rarely made to order. . . .

The drive to the house seemed interminable. She kept her eyes open for a taxi traveling in the opposite direction, but when she pulled in behind the station wagon in the driveway, she was almost sure Drew and Chris hadn't left yet.

An icy wind buffeted her as she hurried toward the house. Inside, Daisy and Buffy came running to greet her. When she noticed Drew's jacket slung over a kitchen chair, a feeling of relief washed over her.

She heard a muffled sound from the floor above. As she made her way upstairs, she fleetingly wondered why she hadn't seen Rags with the other dogs. He was probably with Chris, she thought, as she came to a halt in the bedroom doorway. Drew lifted his suitcase off the bed.

"Thank goodness you're still here," she said.

Drew turned, and from the grim expression on his dark features, she could tell he was still angry.

"What is it? Don't tell me my father has changed his mind," he said in a mocking tone.

"No, he hasn't changed his mind," she said evenly. "But I was hoping I could change yours."

"Leave it, Vienna. You did your best, but you can't perform miracles," he said, carrying the suitcase out into the hallway. "Chris!" Drew called. There was no answer.

"Please, Drew, couldn't you stay until after Christmas?" Vienna asked. "Maybe when Tobias comes home, and you're all together as a family—"

"We're leaving, and that's all there is to say on the matter." Brushing past her, he moved to the top of the stairway. "Chris, come upstairs and give me a hand," he called.

"I didn't see him down there when I came in just now," said Vienna. "I assumed he was up here with you...." Her voice trailed away.

"Of course he's downstairs," Drew countered. "Where else would he be? We came back about an hour ago. When I came upstairs to pack, he was playing in the kitchen with Rags."

"But Rags isn't there, either." Vienna's heart stopped as a terrible thought suddenly rushed into her mind.

Drew must have read the expression on her face, because he disappeared down the stairway at breakneck speed, calling "Chris! Rags!" as he ran. But there was no answer.

Vienna followed and hurried to the back door. She stood outside in the biting wind and scanned the yard, searching for a glimpse of Chris or Rags. Nothing.

When she heard Drew come into the kitchen several minutes later, she closed the door behind her and turned to him.

"He's not in the house. I've looked everywhere," Drew said in a voice that caught at her heart.

"There's no sign of them outside," Vienna said. "But maybe he's just taken Rags for a walk."

"Chris knows not to go out without telling me." Drew impatiently dismissed her suggestion. "If he was outside, he'd be in the yard where we could see him."

There was silence for a long moment, and Vienna saw a look of fear and despair enter his eyes.

"He's run away," Drew said in a throaty whisper, voicing the fear that had already begun to circle in her brain.

Chapter Eleven

"He can't have gone far," Vienna pointed out, alarm clutching at her heart nevertheless. "And Rags is with him."

"I should have anticipated that he'd do something like this." Drew dragged a hand through his hair. "When I picked him up at school and told him we were leaving, he started to cry and said he wanted to stay with you and Gramps and Rags. I tried to explain that he couldn't stay here, that he was my responsibility...." He drew a ragged breath. "Oh, God! What have I done?"

The pain and agony she could hear in Drew's voice brought stinging tears to her eyes.

"Don't do this to yourself, Drew," she said, longing to smooth away the lines of strain on his handsome face. "Chris is angry with you, that's all."

"He has every reason to be," Drew said, as he began to pace the room. "I was too wrapped up in my own anger at my father.... Don't you see? History's repeating itself. Running away was my way of dealing with my anger and frustration eight years ago, and Chris has done the same thing. It's all my fault. If I hadn't been so selfish, so stubborn, I might have realized how all this was affecting my own son. Now he's out there in the freezing cold, all alone.... I've got to find him." He disappeared into the hallway and returned a moment later wearing a red ski jacket.

"I'm coming with you," Vienna declared.

"No. I want you to stay," Drew said in a voice that demanded compliance. "Someone should be here in case he comes back. In fact, you'd better call the police and tell them he's missing."

"You're right," Vienna agreed reluctantly.

When the door closed behind Drew, Vienna crossed to the telephone. She dialed the number of the local police station, but it took some time to convince the sergeant on duty that Chris was missing. Then she had to answer numerous questions. After giving the sergeant a detailed description of the boy, she finally hung up.

Moving to the window, she scanned the driveway and surrounding area, hoping against hope to see Drew returning with Chris, but there was no sign of anyone. She glanced up at the sky, at the dark snow-clouds gathering there, and a shiver of apprehension chased down her spine. Another storm was brewing; it was going to snow heavily. Chris would have to be found—and soon.

Restless and on edge, Vienna turned from the window. She lifted the coffeepot from the stove and began to fill it with water.

In the hour that followed, Vienna pulled on her jacket and opened the back door a dozen times, but after taking only a few steps, she returned to the kitchen, frustrated beyond measure and growing increasingly restless.

At the sound of a car pulling into the driveway, the dogs jumped up and began to bark. Vienna hurried outside, praying that the new arrival was bringing news that Chris and Rags had been found safe and sound.

Her hopes, however were dashed at the sight of Peter Canelli, a young police officer.

"Has he turned up yet?" he asked as she approached.

Vienna shook her head.

"All our patrol cars are on the lookout for the boy," Peter told her, "but so far no one's spotted him."

"I don't think he'll head for town," Vienna said. "I'm sure he's still here somewhere on the property. His father is out looking for him now," she continued, wondering, not for the first time, if Drew had found any trace of the boy.

"If that's the case, maybe I'd better have a couple of units sent out and we'll start a search. I don't like the looks of the sky," he commented.

"Neither do I," Vienna said. "Come inside when you're finished. I've made a pot of coffee."

As Vienna made her way back to the house she noticed, out of the corner of her eye, a figure walking through the orchard toward her. It was Drew.

He was alone.

She ran to meet him, almost falling over herself in her haste.

"Is he here?" Drew asked in a whisper of hope.

She would have given anything to be able to say yes, but she could only shake her head.

A look of pain crossed his features and a bleak expression, the likes of which she'd never seen before, came into his dark eyes. Drew's face was pale and pinched with strain, and it was all she could do not to put her arms around him and offer him comfort.

"I've looked everywhere I can think of," Drew said in a defeated tone. "I found some tracks I was sure were theirs, but after a while they just seemed to go around in circles. I've yelled until I'm almost hoarse, but no one answers...." His voice trailed away, echoing despair.

"The police are here," Vienna told him as they climbed the back steps. "The officer is calling in for reinforcements. They're going to organize a search party."

Once inside, Vienna helped Drew remove his ski jacket and then urged him toward a chair. She poured him a mug of coffee and set it on the table in front of him.

Drew cupped his hands around the mug and took several sips. Vienna watched as color slowly began to creep back into his face.

He was silent for a long moment. Then he pushed the mug aside and dropped his head into his hands. "Where is he?" he said in a hoarse voice. "Dammit, Vienna! Where's my son?" He lifted his head and looked at her with imploring eyes. "If something happens to Chris—" Vienna quickly brought her fingers to his lips to cut off the rest of his words.

"We'll find him," she said confidently. "You have to believe that, Drew."

His hand came up to cover hers and for a fleeting moment, he held it against his chest, as if he were somehow trying to draw strength from her. She could feel the steady rhythm of his heartbeat beneath her fingers, while her own heart beat against her ribs in response. How she loved this man! How she wished she could take away his pain!

Suddenly, the sound of a knock filled the silence. Drew instantly jumped to his feet and flung open the door.

"Mr. Sheridan? I'm Constable Peter Canelli."

"Come in," Drew said, standing aside to let him pass.

"I'm afraid I have nothing new to report, sir. I've just called in and the sergeant is sending out three more officers. Once they arrive, we can begin a proper search of the area. I believe you've already done a preliminary search of your own."

"Yes," Drew said in a tired voice.

"But you found nothing," said the officer.

"I found some footprints I believe were made by my son and the dog. I followed those for a while, but they just seemed to go around in circles."

"Your son has a dog with him?"

"Yes, a golden retriever," Drew said.

"Is it possible, sir, that the boy has just taken the dog for a walk and isn't lost—"

"My son has run away," Drew said in a voice that barely concealed his anger or his pain.

"You're sure of that, sir," persisted the policeman.

"Positive," Drew bit out the word. "And we'll never find him if all you're going to do is ask me foolish questions." He reached for his jacket and strode to the door. "I'm going to look for my son."

"Sir, if you'd wait until the other officers get here . . ." But Drew was already gone.

Peter turned to Vienna and shrugged his shoulders. "I think I'll take a look around outside," he told her. "Sometimes in cases like this, the child is hiding somewhere near the house."

Vienna only nodded. She knew for a fact that if either Chris or Rags were nearby, Buffy and Daisy would be barking. The fact that Chris had taken Rags with him was in his favor. Vienna felt sure that as long as they stayed together, the chances of finding them were far greater than if the boy was alone.

Moments later, she heard the sound of several cars arriving, but before she could go to the window, the telephone rang. She hurried to answer it.

"Hello?"

"Vienna? Is that you?"

"Yes." She was surprised to hear Tobias's voice.

"Have they gone?" Tobias asked anxiously.

"No, they haven't gone," Vienna replied, wondering fleetingly if Tobias had had a change of heart.

"What is it? You sound strange. Is something wrong?" he asked.

"Look, Tobias, I don't want to worry you—" she began.

"Has there been an accident? Is that it?" Tobias was becoming more agitated by the minute.

"No, nothing like that," Vienna quickly assured him. "Chris has run away," she said, deciding that she might upset Tobias more if she tried to avoid his questions.

"Run away? What do you mean?" Tobias asked.

"When he found out Drew was taking him back to San Francisco, he became quite upset. And when Drew went to pack, Chris took Rags and ran away."

"Have you called the police?" Tobias asked urgently.

"Yes, of course," Vienna said. "They're here now."

"And they're out looking for the boy?"

"Yes, everything is under control," she said calmly. "I'll call as soon as he's found. Please, Tobias, try not to worry."

"What else can I do?" Tobias asked, concern in his voice echoing over the line.

"Just pray," Vienna replied, before she replaced the receiver. Glancing at the clock on the wall, she saw that it was almost three-thirty. She grabbed her jacket from the chair. She'd had enough waiting around. She had to do something. "Come on, girls." The dogs ran eagerly to her side. "Let's see if we can find those two."

Outside, it had begun to snow. A gust of cold wind sent flurries dancing around her feet but as Vienna pulled up the hood of her jacket and drew the collar around her face, she tried not to think about how frightened and cold Chris must be.

Daisy bounded off toward the orchard, and Buffy, not to be outdone, raced after her. Thrusting her hands into the pockets of her jacket, Vienna followed.

The world seemed so white and so cold, Vienna thought as she quickened her steps to keep up with the dogs. Over to her left, she saw the three policemen fanned out in a row heading toward the north side of the orchard. One of them saw her and waved.

The path Daisy had chosen was one they'd taken on numerous occasions. It ran through the orchard to an open field on the south. As was Daisy's usual habit, she ran on ahead and then circled back to make sure Vienna was still following. Buffy opted to stay close, and she was glad of the small dog's company. When Vienna reached the narrow stretch of open field, she was in time to see Daisy's black body disappear into woods on the other side, fifty yards away.

The snow was falling thick and fast and visibility was steadily diminishing. Cupping her hands around her mouth Vienna called to Daisy, but the wind quickly whipped the sound away.

With a sigh, Vienna began to cross the field. Buffy, who was finding the trail hard going, stopped and looked up at her.

"I think it's time we turned back," she said as she bent to pick up the small dog. She cupped a hand around her mouth once more and called to Daisy. To her surprise, the dog came running out of the woods, stopping to shake the snow from her coat. Behind her was Drew. He was alone.

At the sight of his drawn, tired features, Vienna felt a sharp and intense pain pierce her heart.

"Any sign of them?" she asked, trying to keep a note of hope in her voice.

"Nothing," he answered. "I don't understand how they could just disappear...."

"You're practically frozen, Drew," Vienna said. "Let's circle back toward the house and see if the policemen have had better luck."

"No, not yet." He shook off her suggestion. Turning, he pointed toward the grove of trees at the far end of the orchard, across the open field.

"I want to take a look in those trees," he said, as Daisy ran back toward them.

"I'll come with you."

Drew nodded, and together they headed in the direction of the cluster of evergreens. Daisy reached them first, and began to bark excitedly at the drooping branches of an evergreen weighted down by the snow.

Suddenly, Vienna heard an answering bark, faint at first, but rapidly growing stronger. Drew came to a halt and Vienna stopped beside him. They stood perfectly still and watched in utter astonishment as Rags, looking rather bedraggled, emerged from among the trees with Chris at his side.

Chris looked ready to drop. His small face was wet with tears and he was clinging to the dog's leash as though it were a lifeline. Rags appeared to be supporting Chris, leading the boy toward them.

Drew was the first to move. With a muffled cry, he ran to his son. Tears of joy slid unheeded down Vienna's cheeks as she watched Drew haul Chris into his arms. With the leash still held tightly in his gloved hand, the boy threw his arms around his father's neck, and Vienna thought she'd never seen a more beautiful sight in her life.

Daisy, still barking, came running toward Vienna. Buffy, undoubtedly wanting to join in this happy reunion, wriggled in Vienna's arms, attempting to jump down. Vienna lowered the dog to the ground. Then she took several steps toward Drew and Chris, hastily wiping the tears from her face as she went.

With Chris still in his arms, Drew reached down to encompass Rags in their embrace. The dog's tail waved from side to side, and Vienna was almost sure Rags was smiling.

"Good dog," Drew said, and glancing up at Vienna, he smiled a smile of pure joy.

"We'd better get Chris back to the house," Vienna said, giving the boy a hug. He looked very cold and very wet. His cheeks were red and the tip of his nose was beginning to turn white. His ski jacket was soaked, and so was his toque.

She reached over to take Rags's leash from him, but he shook his head. "Your dad has to carry you, Chris, and the path is too narrow. You'll end up hurting Rags," she explained. "I'll look after him, I promise." Reluctantly, Chris let her take the leash.

Without further ado, Drew, with Chris held tightly against him, strode off across the open field. Vienna followed at a slower pace. Though Rags was close to exhaustion, the presence of Daisy and Buffy seemed to lift his spirits and renew his energy.

They were more than halfway to the house when they were met by Peter Canelli and another officer. By then, Rags had grown too weary to walk and Vienna was carrying him. Peter offered to take over and she gladly accepted.

"Bring him inside," she instructed as the small troop arrived at the back steps.

Drew had already removed Chris's wet outer-clothes and wrapped him in a warm blanket. He was contentedly seated on his father's knee. His small face broke into a wide smile the moment Peter appeared with Rags and carefully placed him on the floor. "I'll call the station from my patrolcar and pass on the good news," Peter said before he slipped outside.

Wearily, Rags rose to his feet and slowly made his way toward Chris.

"Is he all right?" the boy asked, his eyes filling with tears.

"He's fine," Vienna assured him. "He just needs a good night's rest."

"But his leg, is it okay?" Chris persisted, as he lovingly stroked the golden head.

"As good as new," she told him and was rewarded with a watery smile. "What about you?" she asked. "You had us all worried."

"To put it mildly," Drew said, glancing down at his son.

Chris looked up at his father. "I'm sorry, Dad—" he began in a choked voice. "I didn't mean to walk so far. I got lost in the orchard, and then when I came to the field, I thought the house was on the other side. But I couldn't find my way...." Tears welled up in his eyes as he looked down at the dog. Rags's head was resting on Drew's knee. "I didn't mean to scare you. I was just mad at you 'cause I like it here with Rags and Gramps and Vienna...and you." He stopped and sniffed. "But Rags looked after me. He kept wanting to go the other way and kept pulling me on...."

Vienna felt a lump form in her throat as she watched a solitary tear trickle down Chris's face.

"I guess we have a lot to thank Rags for, and Daisy, too," Drew said softly. He gazed down at his son and swallowed deeply. "All that matters is that you're here and you're safe." He hugged him tightly for several seconds. "I love you, Son."

The words were nothing more than a whisper, but Vienna heard them and her eyes filled with tears.

"I love you too, Dad," Chris said in a muffled voice as he clung to his father.

Vienna smiled and, glancing at Drew, saw a glint of tears in his eyes.

"There are some things we need to talk about," Drew began, as he eased himself away from Chris. "I'm not angry with you for running away." At his words, Vienna saw a look of relief flash across the boy's features. "I understand why you did it, because I ran away from home, too."

Chris's eyes widened in surprise. "You did?"

"Yes," Drew replied softly. "I was much older than you, and I should have known better...."

"Why did you run away?" Chris asked.

"Because I was angry at my father."

"What were you angry about?" Chris's eyes were intent on his father's face.

"Although I was over twenty-one, my father was still treating me like a child—telling me what to do, when to do it, who my friends should be...." Drew's voice trailed off, and he glanced fleetingly at Vienna before continuing. "When I tried to tell him what I wanted to do with my life, he refused to listen."

"That wasn't fair," Chris said.

At his words, Drew smiled. "No, you're right, it wasn't fair," he agreed. "But I haven't exactly been fair to you, either. We came here because I wanted to try to patch things up with your grandfather, but we were both too stubborn to give an inch, and you were caught in the middle. And when your grandfather refused to accept my help today, I got angry with him all over again.

"I realize now that I should have taken the time to explain to you why we couldn't stay, but instead, I completely ignored your feelings. That was wrong of me. I'm sorry, Chris. But I haven't been a father very long, and I'm just beginning to find out what a tough job it is."

Vienna saw Chris frown, as if he were trying to sort out all Drew had said. "Maybe Gramps found it tough to be a father, too," he said.

Drew stared at his son for a long moment. "I hadn't thought of that."

Suddenly the door opened and Peter Canelli reappeared. "Excuse me, sir. I called the station and told them that the boy's all right, but the sergeant thinks it might be wise to have him checked over by a doctor. We can easily run you to the hospital."

"That's a good idea," Drew said.

"Do I have to?" Chris asked.

"Yes," replied his father, and lifting Chris into his arms, he stood.

"But Rags—" Chris protested.

"I'll stay with Rags," Vienna quickly intervened. "Oh, and Drew—I forgot to tell you that Tobias called a little while ago. He knows Chris was missing. While you're at the hospital, why don't you stop in and tell him everything's all right?"

Drew's dark eyes held hers for a breathless second. A flicker of emotion—an emotion she couldn't define—danced briefly in their depths.

"The patrolcar's all warmed up, sir," Peter announced.

Drew turned and, pulling the blanket around Chris, followed Peter Canelli outside.

Vienna slowly released the breath she'd been holding and closed her eyes tightly. As she'd listened to Drew talk to Chris, she'd heard a new understanding in his voice, and her heart had overflowed with love for him.

Terrifying as Chris's disappearance had been, it had obviously jolted Drew into an awareness of just how precious his son was to him, and just how much he had to lose. That he loved Chris was irrefutable and Vienna could only hope that for Chris's sake, Drew might be willing to talk to Tobias one more time.

A cold nose nudged at her hand. Vienna opened her eyes and looked down at Rags. "Well, you certainly turned out to be quite a hero," she murmured, crouching down to stroke the dog's head. "I'll bet after all that work, you're hungry."

Daisy and Buffy suddenly pushed against her, almost knocking her over. "All right, I guess you deserve a treat, too," she said to them, a hint of laughter in her voice now.

Once the dogs were fed, they lay contentedly in their favorite spots on the kitchen floor. Beginning to feel hungry herself, Vienna decided to keep busy by cooking up a pot of spaghetti.

Outside, it had stopped snowing. As she worked, her eyes constantly flicked to the clock on the wall. The hands seemed to be moving at a snail's pace. Vienna found her thoughts returning to that moment in the kitchen when Drew had told Chris that he loved him.

A pain stabbed in Vienna's heart as she felt an acute longing to hear Drew say the same words to her. Why did loving someone have to hurt so much?

She tried not to think that there was still a strong possibility Drew and Chris would be leaving in the morning. She blinked back the tears suddenly stinging her eyes and tried unsuccessfully to convince herself that if Drew and Chris did leave, she would survive . . . somehow.

She glanced at the clock for the hundredth time. It was six-fifteen. The sauce for the spaghetti bubbled away on the stove and the noodles were ready and waiting.

Where were they? Had Drew gone to see Tobias? Perhaps the doctors had suggested that Chris spend the night at the hospital. But surely Drew would have called?

The crunch of a car's tires in the driveway brought the dogs to their feet, and amid their riotous barking Vienna hurried to the window. It was a police car. When the rear door opened and Drew climbed out, the relief and joy that swept through her almost made her faint.

As she opened the door for them, she willed her heart to stop its frantic pounding. When Drew appeared, carrying Chris, it was all she could do not to throw herself at them both.

"You're back," she managed a little breathlessly.

"Dr. McGregor checked me over and said I was fine," Chris informed her as Drew lowered him to the floor where he was instantly bowled over by Rags.

At the mention of Bruce, Vienna felt her heart drop to her toes. Her eyes flew to Drew's face but his expression was unreadable.

"I made spaghetti," Vienna said, sure that Drew must hear her heart hammering against her breastbone. "I hope you're both hungry."

"I'm starving," Drew confirmed, and as he spoke, his glance captured hers and a spasm of need, like a bolt of lightning, shot through her. It took every ounce of strength she possessed to drag her eyes from his. She turned toward the stove and bit down on her lower lip to stop herself from crying out.

"Rags, you're tickling me," Chris said, laughing.

Vienna glanced down at Chris, still fighting to suppress the ache of longing tearing through her. It wasn't fair that with one look Drew could ignite a fire deep inside her that threatened to annihilate what little control she had left.

Chris looked up at his father and smiled. "Can I tell Vienna, Dad?"

"Tell me what?" she asked, deliberately keeping her eyes on Chris, but aware—oh, so aware—of the man standing only a few feet behind her.

"That we're staying for Christmas," said Chris, his eyes glinting with excitement—and something else.

Her heart skipped a beat. "That's great!" said Vienna. "I'm really glad."

"Gramps insisted," Chris went on, standing and moving toward the hallway. At his words, Vienna swiftly brought her eyes back to Drew's in time to see a conspiratorial glance pass between father and son.

"So you did go and see Tobias," she said. Puzzled, she watched as Chris made a hasty exit.

"Yes, I saw him. While your good friend Dr. McGregor examined Chris," he said evenly.

"And..." Vienna prompted.

Drew smiled, and the action sent her heart into a tailspin. "We talked, Vienna—we really talked!" There was a warmth and satisfaction in his tone that made Vienna smile, too.

"And..."

"My father and I are now in partnership—"

Vienna let out a whoop of joy and threw herself into his arms, forgetting everything but the fact that

Drew's relationship with Tobias had taken a giant step forward.

Suddenly, the realization that she was in Drew's arms hit her and hastily she began to pull away. "I'm sorry," she mumbled against his sweater, but Drew tightened his hold, making it impossible for her to leave the haven of his arms.

The rich, dark, male scent of him teased her nostrils, and she discovered that her lips were only a scant few inches from the curve of his neck. Her legs suddenly felt as weak as a newborn foal's, and for a moment she wondered if she was dreaming.

"I also had a brief talk with Dr. McGregor." Drew's voice was low, and his lips brushed the hair at her ear, leaving a trail of fire behind.

Vienna swallowed and lifted her face to look at him. "You did?"

"I did," Drew repeated, and she saw a flicker of heat come and go in his eyes before he continued. "He told me that he didn't appreciate losing out to me."

Drew's nearness was making it increasingly difficult for Vienna to concentrate on what he was saying. Somehow her hands had found their way around his waist, and the feel of his muscular back beneath her fingers was doing strange things to her breathing.

"When I asked him what he meant," Drew continued, his breath fanning her like a gentle caress, "he said that you weren't going to marry him, because you were in love with me."

Vienna gasped and tried to pull away, but Drew easily stilled her frantic struggles.

"Drew, please let me go," Vienna pleaded. He was laughing at her, she was sure of it, and she couldn't bear it.

"Is it true?" he asked, and at the note of hope in his voice her heart stopped beating, then relentlessly gathered speed.

Vienna lifted her head to look at Drew and noticed instantly the tension etched on his face. She watched in fascination as a nerve jumped at the edge of his jaw. When she lifted her gaze to meet his, there was no mistaking his look of fear.

But what was he afraid of? Was he afraid she'd say "Yes" or afraid she'd say "No"? Taking a deep, steadying breath, she decided to throw caution to the wind.

"Yes, it's true." The words were a gift, a promise, a dream come true, and when his mouth came unerringly down on hers, she felt as if she'd come home at last—come home after a long and painful journey.

There was no tenderness in his kiss, but she wanted none. There would be time enough for tenderness. And as his lips plundered hers, she responded with all the love in her heart. This was what she'd dreamed of, longed for from the moment he'd arrived on the doorstep.

She could taste his need and as it mingled with her own, the heat that swept through her increased and intensified until she thought she would explode.

He was hers—she knew it in every cell of her body and in every corner of her heart; and that knowledge alone was the greatest gift he could ever give her.

Slowly, gently, the urgency drained from them both and when his mouth left hers, Vienna knew she would be content to have him hold her like this forever.

"Tell me I'm not dreaming," Drew said, his voice a husky whisper of emotion.

She couldn't speak, so she kissed his mouth once more.

"You've given me so much already, I hardly dared to hope," he said, gazing down at her with eyes that reflected the fire burning inside her. "Tell me you love me," he ordered her in a voice that trembled with suppressed emotion. "I need to hear you say the words."

"I love you, Drew," she said without hesitation. "I think I always have." Her heart was overflowing.

His arms tightened around her and she felt the last of the tension in his body slip away.

"When you opened the door the night Chris and I arrived, I felt as if I'd been hit by a train," he said softly. "I hadn't realized until the moment I saw you just how much I wanted to come home for good. And each time I looked at you, each time I kissed you, I lost another piece of my heart. I want nothing more than to spend the rest of my life here, with you and Chris. I know he'll approve. But what about you? Do you think you can cope with two more stubborn Sheridan men?" His lips brushed her hair and she could feel his heart pounding at a speed that matched her own.

"I'm rather partial to proud, stubborn, men, especially if they happen to be Sheridans," Vienna said, love and laughter bubbling in her voice now.

"Is that a yes?"

"That's a yes," Vienna confirmed, happiness welling up inside her. "Let's tell Chris."

"Tell me what?" Chris asked, reappearing in the doorway.

"That we're staying for Christmas...and for always," said Drew.

"All right!" Chris shouted. At the sudden sound, Rags began to bark. Seconds later Buffy and Daisy joined in.

"Tobias said they'd be releasing him from the hospital in a few days," Drew said, when the noise began to subside.

"Just in time for Christmas," Chris said, smiling up at them.

"I think it's going to be the best Christmas ever," Vienna said on a sigh. And as she raised her lips to Drew's, she knew that the love she'd yearned for and dreamed about for so long was hers at last.

* * * * *

DIAMOND JUBILEE CELEBRATION!

It's the Silhouette Books tenth anniversary, and what better way to celebrate than to toast *you*, our readers, for making it all possible. Each month in 1990 we presented you with a DIAMOND JUBILEE Silhouette Romance written by an all-time favorite author! Saying thanks has never been so romantic....

If you missed any of the DIAMOND JUBILEE Silhouette Romances, order them by sending your name, address, zip or postal code, along with a check or money order for $2.25 for each book ordered, plus 75¢ for postage and handling, payable to Silhouette Reader Service to:

In the U.S.	In Canada
3010 Walden Ave.,	P.O. Box 609
P.O. Box 1396	Fort Erie, Ontario
Buffalo, NY 14269-1396	L2A 5X3

Please specify book title(s) with your order.

January:	ETHAN by Diana Palmer (#694)
February:	THE AMBASSADOR'S DAUGHTER by Brittany Young (#700)
March:	NEVER ON SUNDAE by Rita Rainville (#706)
April:	HARVEY'S MISSING by Peggy Webb (#712)
May:	SECOND TIME LUCKY by Victoria Glenn (#718)
June:	CIMARRON KNIGHT by Pepper Adams (#724)
July:	BORROWED BABY by Marie Ferrarella (#730)
August:	VIRGIN TERRITORY by Suzanne Carey (#736)
September:	MARRIED?! by Annette Broadrick (#742)
	THE HOMING INSTINCT by Dixie Browning (#747)
October:	GENTLE AS A LAMB by Stella Bagwell (#748)
November:	SONG OF THE LORELEI by Lucy Gordon (#754)
December:	ONLY THE NANNY KNOWS FOR SURE by Phyllis Halldorson (#760)

Hurry! Quantities are limited.

SRJUB-1AAA

You'll flip . . . your pages won't!
Read paperbacks *hands-free* with

Book Mate · I

The perfect "mate" for all your romance paperbacks

**Traveling • Vacationing • At Work • In Bed • Studying
• Cooking • Eating**

Perfect size for all standard paperbacks, this wonderful invention makes reading a pure pleasure! Ingenious design holds paperback books OPEN and FLAT so even wind can't ruffle pages — leaves your hands free to do other things. Reinforced, wipe-clean vinyl-covered holder flexes to let you turn pages without undoing the strap . . . supports paperbacks so well, they have the strength of hardcovers!

Pages turn WITHOUT opening the strap

SEE-THROUGH STRAP

Reinforced back stays flat

Built in bookmark

BOOK MARK

BACK COVER
HOLDING STRIP

10 x 7¼ opened
Snaps closed for easy carrying, too

WRITTEN IN THE STARS

Star-crossed lovers?
Or a match made in heaven?

Why are some heroes strong and silent . . . and
others charming and cheerful? The answer is
WRITTEN IN THE STARS! Coming each
month in 1991, Silhouette Romance presents
you with a special love story written by one of
your favorite authors—highlighting the hero's
astrological sign! From January's sensible
Capricorn to December's disarming Sagittarius,
you'll meet a dozen dazzling heroes.

Sexy, serious Justin Starbuck wasn't about to be
tempted by his aunt's lovely hired companion,
but Philadelphia Jones thought his love life
needed her helping hand! What happens when
this cool, conservative Capricorn meets his
match in a sweet, spirited blonde like
Philadelphia?